The Document Matters

ABC Group Documentation //
878 Mallory Drive
Marietta, GA 30062

Grateful acknoweldgment is made by the author to the editors of the following publications, where these stories first appeared.

"Creepy" appeared in *Beat to a Pulp,* 2017. "Atomic Fuel" appeared in *The Digest Enthusiast,* 2017. "Sidewalk Flowers" appeared in *MicroHorror,* 2018. "Emuq" appeared in *Massacre Magazine,* 2017. "Broke" appeared in *Horror Bites,* 2018. "Useful Things" appeared in *EconoClash Review,* 2018. "Worms" appeared in *Indiana Horror Review,* 2015.

ISBN: 978-1-64396-067-8

Printed in the USA.

LAKE COUNTY INCIDENTS

by

Alec Cizak

Acknowledgements:

I am forever in debt to my wife, Yuan, for her tireless work as my first reader and proofreader. She also serves as critic, advisor, and my biggest supporter. I would also like to thank Mav Skye for the time she's taken not only on this project, but over the past decade or so, to read and comment on my work. Additionally, I'd like to thank Jeremy Stabile and ABC Group Documentation for taking risks on books that collide with the mainstream. Hopefully, history will prove those risks necessary and worth it.

Dedicated to Dad, who read Poe stories to me
before bedtime at an entirely inappropriate age.

CONTENTS

CREEPY

We checked on the van in the back of the Walmart parking lot shortly after the second body surfaced near Turkey Creek. Not too far from the first corpse, which had been discovered the previous week. Both victims were female. College students from Valpo. Dark hair. Mini-skirts. Too much makeup. Disappeared after a night of boozing. None of us believed we'd ever harbor a serial killer in little old Lublin, Indiana. That sort of thing just didn't happen around here. We got to discussing the problem at the Pub 900.

Dale Kipple, who lost his legs in Desert Storm, fixed foreign cars at a shop in Merrillville, and once ran for mayor as a libertarian, said, "I know everyone on Fifth Street. Not a soul there capable of taking another human life."

His hunting buddy, Jack Houck, a professed vegetarian who owned and ran the deli on Temple Avenue, echoed his friend's sentiment—"I've lived in Lublin my entire life. Ain't ever met anyone so freaky they'd commit murder."

Most of us agreed the university in Valpo had attracted undesirable characters over the years. Their shenanigans usually involved drinking too much and the occasional rape of a student or professor who'd passed out in the street.

Several nights of debate led to the obvious conclusion that the Turkey Creek Killer, as the *Free Press* had taken to calling him, her, or it, could not be someone local. We were church-going folk. Most of us were Lutheran. A few were Catholics, but we forgave them. Politically, we leaned toward the right, though there were a good number of liberals amongst us who, as predicted, suggested we not rush to judgment.

Dennis Cromwell fell on that side of the fence. He taught something called "gender studies" at Valpo and rumor had it he apologized to his students at the beginning of every semester for having been born with testicles instead of ovaries. We didn't much prefer the kind of talk folks like Dennis produced, but he'd lived here several decades with his chunky wife Ellen and we'd gotten used to hearing him tell us all manner of ways up was down and day was night and so on. You've watched television recently, been to the movies, listened to the monotonous bile passing for pop music, you know what we're getting at...Dennis said, "Obviously, a very disturbed misogynist has found his way to Lublin. Before we condemn him, let's find out what his father did to him when he was a child."

We suggested Dennis head to the Dollar Store on Madison Avenue and buy an ounce of common sense.

Then a third body snagged Jeff Coe's fishing line. He'd cast under the bridge near the old train station by the creek. Sat in the autumn sun drinking beer and complaining to his buddy Zach Park about some Somalis who'd moved in to the house next to his. Said it was only a matter of time before ISIS convinced his new neighbors to go on some sort of holy rampage. Jeff might have been a little bonkers from his days as a foreman at Werner's dairy farm, but he sure looked humble when he described pulling in the bloated corpse of a Valpo girl named Melissa Larsen. Dark hair, brown eyes. Known at the Pub 900 for playing poker and getting soused every Wednesday night.

"That woman was naked as the day God sent her from her Mama's womb," he told us. "Thought for sure I'd caught a fifty-pounder, something I might be able to sell at the farmer's market on Sunday." He said he struggled, tugging on the line, until he swallowed his pride and asked his buddy Zach to help him. They dragged the girl's tattered body onto the rocks. Zach called Lublin PD. They finished their beer waiting for them to show.

"Going to be a long time," said Jeff, "before I get to sleep without seeing that girl's wide eyes staring at me like I was the one who snuffed her."

We asked about the wound in her throat. "Oh, it was cut all right," he said. "Ripped open like a bag of cereal."

Once the local police were convinced the three murders were the work of the same deranged individual, they contacted the FBI. Enough of us loitered in and around the station to learn bits and pieces: The young women had been violated before and after their throats had been slit. Coroner they brought in from D.C. said the wounds were so jagged and rough, the killer must have used a rusted blade.

Black SUVs with D.C. plates roamed Lublin for three days like predators. The women called them "creepy," said maybe we'd let Big Brother a little too close. Said we should be able to weed out the killer ourselves.

"Take away the students who rent rooms during the school year," said Mrs. Lacy, who ran a group home near the bus depot on Temple Avenue, "and what kind of population we got here?" She pushed up the sleeves on her thick, wool sweater and answered before anyone else could—"Not much, I tell you, that's what we got here. Not much. What's it going to take to figure out who doesn't belong?" She paused, as though we could read her mind. "Not much," she said, "it's not going to take much."

The women insisted we form our own teams to fan out and investigate. Good thing, too. The FBI lollygagged a couple of days and announced they were returning to D.C. to run tests and conjecture and do all manner of things unrelated to picking through strangers in Lublin to figure out who was round and who was square.

Most of us found nothing out of place, nothing beyond usual. Frank Gosch and his wife Sue, however, arrived at the pub with the most astonishing news. They'd spent the day scouring the mall and the Walmart on Madison Avenue. After chatting with pretty little Katie Romero, who welcomed folks at the door of the Walmart, they learned a white van with Missouri license plates had been parking overnight in the Walmart lot for almost a month.

"Oh, you better believe Katie's concerned," said Frank. "She even called the police. They interviewed the guy who sleeps in the van and told her the only thing they could do is fine him for loitering." We shook our heads. Lublin cops were notorious for being next to useless when things got serious. They were never around when drunks downtown started bar fights. They always showed up afterward, when the men were finished bashing in each other's brains and had gone back to killing themselves the more civilized way—whiskey and beer. We decided to take a trip to the Walmart and have a chat with the gentleman in the van.

Turned out to be a 120, no windows on the side. Every movie and TV show we'd ever seen about serial killers, vans always played a role. Ron Stork, bus driver for the Lake County School District and Lublin's dead-ringer for Grizzly Adams, tapped on the side of it. "Open up," he said. We knew someone was home. Flashing blue lights inside suggested the man had a small television. He poked his head out.

"Yes?" he said with an air as pompous as a savior.

"We'd like to talk with you," said Dale Kipple.

The stranger stepped from the van. Couldn't have been more than five-foot two. Balding, wore spectacles. His collared t-shirt and blue jeans looked like they hadn't seen a laundry machine in ages. And he smelled. He smelled bad, like he'd made a career of soiling his drawers and refusing to wash them.

We didn't need too much more. This was our guy.

But Sue Gosch, at the prompt of Dennis Cromwell, proceeded to interrogate him anyway. "We'd like to know who you are and what your business is in Lublin." She folded her arms across her well-endowed chest.

He drew his face back, as though he'd gotten a whiff of himself for the first time. "Beg pardon?" You'd have thought he was the Pope and answered to no one other than God.

"Katie Romero says you've been parking here a month," said Sue. "You planning on living here forever, or you going to move on some time?"

The stranger said, "Manager of the Walmart told me I could crash here provided I don't bother nobody."

We were stunned. Lou Papelini ran the Walmart. He hadn't lived in Lublin for too long. He had a black, curly head of hair that always made us a little nervous. Surely he must have had better sense than to let a drifter take residence in his lot.

Sue motioned for us to keep quiet. She taught kindergarten at Haggard Elementary, knew how to control a rowdy situation. "Mister," she said, "I think we'd feel a lot better if you'd mosey on to another town."

You'd have thought the stranger was Jesus, the way he took offense to her suggestion. "I beg your pardon," he said again. "Last time I checked, this was a free country."

Oh boy. We looked at each other, we shook our heads, sighed, made clicking sounds with our tongues. Wasn't this the go-to excuse for strangers and weirdoes everywhere? People who didn't fit in always tried that bit, never understanding freedom only belonged to normal folks, like us.

Frank Gosch said, "Look, buddy, we don't want to cast nasty aspersions, but we've had some trouble and we'd like to eighty-six any possible culprits." He nodded his square jaw like one of those tough guy lawyers we always saw on television.

The stranger smirked and got back into his van. Before he slammed the side doors, he said, "Bug me again, I'll sick the cops on you."

That gave us a hardy-har-har. We couldn't get the police to toss him out of town and he thought they'd actually give a darn about *his* rights? One thing was clear:

The man was creepy. The women used that word over and over to describe him:

"Did you see the clothes he was wearing?"

Creepy.

"He looked just like that serial killer from Chicago, you remember the clown in the ice cream truck?"

Creepy!

"My God, he reminded me of a short, fat, balding Ed Gein!"

Creepy!!!

We invited Sergeant Alphonse Booker to the pub the following night. He was a local boy. Played football for Gary South the year they came within three games of state. We thought we could trust him. We said, "Sergeant, you got to escort that stranger right out of town."

"Unless Lou Papelini tells me otherwise," he said, "the man is welcome to park his van and sleep there."

The women chimed in, said he looked creepy and they just *knew* he was the Turkey Creek Killer.

"You see anything in his van to make you think so?"

We hadn't done a spectacular job of investigating. Most of us felt no need. The stranger was clearly a weirdo. Only weirdoes committed murder. Hell, any television show about criminals would confirm that.

The sergeant told us not to get involved. "You let the authorities take care of this from here on." We asked just what they were doing to fix the problem. He said, "We're waiting on Uncle Sam to get back with the lab results."

We rolled our eyes at that one. Surely the sergeant knew better than to trust the government! He said nabbing serial killers fell under federal jurisdiction. Then he said, "You all don't pay me enough to mount a serious investigation anyway."

He was shown the door at that point. We decided to head on back over to Madison Avenue and give the stranger in the van another look. We needed to find some good evidence. When we got to his spot near the rear of the Walmart parking lot, his windshield flashed blue and white again. We banged on the side doors until he showed his arrogant face. Dan Gruber, football coach at Haggard High, three-hundred and fifty pounds, hands the size of baseball mitts, dragged him out and held him against the van by his throat. The rest of us jumped inside and went through the garbage he'd collected. There were no benches, just blankets and trash bags. His tiny television, a black and white number from the last century, sat on the hump between the front seats. He had no antenna. He was watching static. *Creepy.* We found a paper sack from a grocery store we'd never heard of filled with plastic knives, forks, and spoons. Inside half a pack of Styrofoam plates, he'd wedged a steak knife.

A *real* steak knife.

Some of us argued—"Remember, the coroner said it was rusty."

The rest of us got them to go along—"It's a knife, ain't it?"

We pointed out tiny, red stains on the jagged teeth of the blade.

"Could be catsup," said one wise guy.

We glared at him until he caved.

We shoved the knife in the stranger's face.

"Yeah?" He spoke in snotty tones we'd have expected from a teenager.

"Looks like a murder weapon to me," said Carl Gooseberg, the near-sighted owner of the shooting range in Hammond.

The stranger chuckled. Only a creepy, weirdo psychopath would laugh when confronted with that kind of evidence.

"We're taking you downtown," said Dan. "Cops won't come and get you, we'll bring you to them." He bunched the stranger's dirty t-shirt around his fist.

The stranger dropped to the ground, refused to go.

"Going to need some help," said Dan.

So we grabbed the stranger wherever we could and dragged him across the concrete. He screamed for his life, claimed he was being abducted. Funny how you let relativism fester long enough, evil will call itself a victim.

He made himself heavy as a sack of wet concrete. We lost our grips and had to pull him with more force, smacking his head against the pavement, over and over, until we noticed he'd stopped making noise, stopped moving, stopped resisting.

"Hey," Dan said to him.

We dropped him, offered him the chance to escape, to prove to us he was still alive. His creepy brown eyes stared at us in the cold, blue moonlight. His mouth had twisted and wouldn't untwist. Dale Kipple leaned in close, put his ear near his chest.

"Friends," he said, "he found the best way to escape justice."

We agreed to leave him there. Let the lazy police see if they could figure out what had happened to him. We told the women we'd spotted the murder weapon and that's all they needed to know. Hell, they'd assumed the man guilty long before we did.

Lublin's finest wrote off the stranger's death as a heart attack. Who knew? Who cared? Just days after he died, we met a girl from Valpo at Pub 900 on college night. Her name was Sadie. She had long, gorgeous black hair, wore glitter on her face like a pop star. We watched her drink six mugs of beer. We liked her. We really,

really liked her. We waited for her in the alley behind the bar. She stepped outside around one in the morning to toss her cookies near a green dumpster. She was alone. We *loved* that. We put our hands around her mouth and carried her into the darkness.

CANCERS

Danuta Kava parked in the alley on the side of her parent's house. The two-story castle she'd grown up in seemed small enough to hold in her hands. Dirt had caked onto the white, aluminum siding and wet leaves spilled from the thin gutters. She grabbed her purse and locked her rental car. She hadn't returned to Haggard since leaving twenty-five years ago for Los Angeles. Her mother had called her stupid, promised she'd become just another "whore of Babylon" out there "amongst the filth." Her father predicted she'd get hooked on dope and die in a gutter.

Concrete steps leading to the front door had crumbled from neglect. The steel railing she'd slid down on her way to school when she was a girl had come loose and threatened to spill to the side. She waited for her sister, Kristyna, who had the keys.

Her sister never left town. She taught history at Haggard High. They hadn't spoken since she sent Danuta a nasty card after their father's death. Danuta's husband Enrique had been in the middle of a reelection campaign. She used his career as an excuse to skip the formal goodbye to the man who'd once called her his Grand Disappointment. Kristyna asked her why she hadn't visited him in the hospital. "As much as you hate him," she'd written, "you might have gotten a kick, seeing the cancer eat him from the inside out."

A battered Ford station wagon from the last century pulled in behind Danuta's shiny rental. Her sister opened the creaky driver's side door and eased herself out. Her turquois Mumu made her look like a giant bullet. Acne from her awkward teen years had left craters and scars on her face. Danuta scolded herself for noticing. Living in California had made her shallow. "It's been so long," she said. She held her arms open, expected time and the loss of their mother to drain the moat of contempt between them.

Her sister gave her a quick hug and patted her on the back. "*Dani.*" All business. No love. She moved around her, opened the torn screen door, and slid a key into the bolt lock.

Danuta followed her into the house. The living room smelled like Band-Aids and stale fabric. Nothing had changed. Same pumpkin-colored couch, same mismatched loveseats, even the same television. "This still work?" She fiddled with rabbit ears set on top of a VCR next to it.

Kristyna flipped a light in the kitchen and asked her if she needed anything to drink.

"No thanks." She walked through the dining room, stared at the oval, extension table in the center. Memories of trying to digest dinner while her father grilled her about her day at school twisted her nerves. He stood over her and Kristyna at that same table, forcing them to study two hours a night. He assured them they'd amount to nothing if they didn't make decent grades.

Kristyna cussed about the refrigerator being empty. She found a can of V8 and popped the lid. "You can stay in your old room, if you want." She faced a picture window overlooking Lake Arthur, just beyond the back yard. "Mom never messed with it. Pretty sure your posters of Chris Cornell are still on the walls. Well, most of them. I took the one of him screaming into a microphone. You left so much here, you know, when you left."

"I thought you wanted to go through the house and decide what we'd keep and what we'd sell?" said Danuta.

Her sister sighed. "Is that all you came for?" She started for their father's study, a small room to the left of the dining room, near the foot of the stairs. "You going to skip Mom's funeral, too?"

"Give me a break." Danuta sat on one of two round, leather seats near her father's bookshelf. Dust coated multiple versions of the Bible and other religious texts.

Her sister took the office chair in front of her father's desk and woke a slumbering computer surrounded by papers and manila folders. "Mom thought she'd have more time. She kept telling her doctor she thought something was wrong with her stomach. He just fed her more pills."

Danuta said, "Does that thing have Internet?"

"Mom was pretty active on Facebook, if you can believe it."

"What are you doing on there, anyway?"

"Mom made a list of who gets what," said Kristyna.

"Mind if I check my email?"

"By all means. Take care of yourself first, Dani." She moved out of the way.

Danuta set her purse next to the computer. She leaned over the desk and clicked through several opened browsers. She stopped at a satellite image of the Grand Canyon. "Well, well," she said. She zoomed in, then zoomed out. "Thought I'd see if this thing was sharp enough to pick up people on donkeys."

Kristyna put her hand over her mouth.

"It's okay to laugh," said Danuta. "Mom was old. We all go, sooner or later."

"Jesus, Dani." Her sister frowned. "The woman's not even in the ground."

"All right, all right." She clicked the search history on the satellite page. A list dropped down. She read it out loud—"Yellowstone… Devil's Tower…the Badlands…"

Her sister cleared her throat. "She liked looking at places we went on vacation. You know, when we were little, when Dad's job paid him enough to take us on the road for a couple of weeks."

"Those were the days." Danuta clicked the search box. "Want to see my house in Santa Barbara?" She typed in her California address. The satellite drew back, into outer space, and zeroed in on the west coast, zooming all the way to the very tops of the houses in her neighborhood. She tilted the image until the front of her villa came into view. "What do you think?"

Her sister said, "Neat."

"How about your place?" She erased her Santa Barbara address and waited for Kristyna to tell her exactly where she lived in Haggard.

"You could come by and see it in person."

"I plan to, Kristy, don't worry."

"I mean," she said, "you could have just asked. You could have stayed with me and Mark."

Danuta held her breath. "I didn't think you'd want me to." She stared at framed photos on the windowsill. The sun had bleached them, washed out the colors. In a shot of her and her sister, maybe when she was seven and her sister was three, sharing a swing at Washington Park, her sister rested her head on her shoulder, her eyes aimed at her in awe.

"Whatever," said Kristyna.

"Okay." Danuta looked at the blank search field on the screen. "I got an idea." She typed her parents' address. "Let's see if the satellite is watching us right now." The image drew back into space, then zoomed into northern Indiana and settled right over the house. "Look," she said, "there's your station wagon."

Kristyna rested her palm on the desk and squinted. "Where's your car?"

"Oh," said Danuta. "This must be from the past."

"Probably." Kristyna headed for the stairs. "The Ford used to be Mom's. I bought it from her when she stopped driving. That was, wow, three years ago."

Danuta clicked to a different angle. "Guess these street pictures aren't so new." She looked at the front of the house. The stoop and railing weren't as deteriorated. She rotated the image to see the other side, the side facing the lake. The windows from her parents' bedroom were almost dark. In the lower right corner of the window to the left, a white smudge, like a splash of snow, caught her attention. "What's that?"

Her sister sighed and walked back into the room. She peered over her shoulder. "Let's head upstairs, make sure your bed's okay."

Danuta leaned in closer. The white smudge on the window looked like a face with long, narrow black eyes, elongated nostrils, and a wide-open mouth. "Freaky," she said.

She joined her sister and climbed the winding, awkward stairs to the second floor. The wood underneath the frayed carpet creaked with each step. The door to their parents' bedroom was closed. Her sister's room had no door. Neither did hers. She asked what had happened.

"They made too much noise at night," said Kristyna. "Mom had Mark take them off and put them in the cellar."

Danuta stepped into her old room. Her brass bed shined in the sunlight beaming through the only window. The rafters above shifted and groaned.

Her sister shook her head. "Old houses are like old people. Their bones ache and they complain a lot." She wiped her finger on the bedspread. "Wow," she said. "Mom must have washed your sheets and made the bed before she went into the hospital." She looked at her. "Maybe she knew you'd opt to crash here and not with me."

"Bowel cancer?"

"Seeing as how they both got the Big C," said Kristyna, "no reason to think you and I shouldn't be on the lookout."

Danuta shrugged. "I get a full screening every year."

"Must be nice." Her sister patted the pillow on her bed. "You might want to order out for food. Not much in the kitchen." She started for the stairs.

"You're leaving?"

"Mark's watching the kids," she said. "I don't get home soon, no telling what he'll let them have for dinner."

"Oh," said Danuta. She couldn't admit she didn't want to be alone. Some primitive desire to look as tough as she was when they were growing up. What would her sister think? She used to give her noogies until she ran to her mother crying. How could a bully like her fear a house? "Well," she said, "let's go to the service together, tomorrow, cool?"

Her sister smiled and bowed her head. "I'll come by at eleven-thirty."

"Great." Danuta followed her down the stairs and through the living room. She said goodbye to her three times before her sister got into her station wagon and drove toward Eighth Street. She stayed on the crumbling front stoop, nudging loose clunks of concrete with the toe of her shoe. The house, looming behind her, felt like a stranger, a stalker, even. An autumn wind barreled through, pestered naked branches on a pair of oak trees at the foot of the driveway. She grabbed her arms and stepped back in.

She locked the door and hustled to the study. She hadn't eaten since the flight. She'd take her sister's advice, order a pizza, and plop down on a loveseat in the living room and see if the television still picked up Channel 9 from Chicago. She sat at the computer and looked at the dated image of her parents' house on the satellite page. She examined the white smudge in the window. Still seemed a desperate, angry face. But, hadn't it been on the left side? She opened a new browser, dismissed her concern as the result of an aging mind with diminished short-term memory. She Googled Dominoes and ordered a medium with peppers and onions. She went back to the satellite page. She swiveled the image up and down, back and forth. The eyes of the smudge never moved. The floorboards from the upstairs hallway moaned, as though someone were walking on them. Her shoulders shook against her will. She grabbed her purse and moved to the living room, hoped the TV would do its job and quell her imagination.

A high-pitched hum from the television's tube suggested something in it still worked. A pin of light developed in the center of the screen and expanded to static. She adjusted the rabbit ears and flipped through the channels. Nothing. The antenna had not been updated for the change to digital. She pressed the power button on the VCR next to the television. She opened cabinets in the TV stand and found videotapes with barely legible labels— *Winter, 1983*; *Christmas, 1982*; *Summer, 1984*. She shoved a tape in, rewound it, and pressed play. The first few minutes had been filmed inside St. Bridget's during service. The whine from the engine of the camera drowned most of the other sounds. At one point, the priest—she couldn't remember his name now—walked over and asked her father just what he thought he was doing. The scene changed to the back yard, in front of Lake Arthur. She and her sister wore their blue and white Sunday dresses. Little Kristyna had to be three or four. Her hair had been tied into Cindy Brady pigtails. She ran through their mother's garden with a cheap, plastic Easter basket on her arm. Danuta, much taller, followed her. Hearing her little sister laugh every time she discovered another colored egg under a rock or near a tree forced her to smile. Not long after whenever the video had been made, she'd started bullying Kristyna every day. Her father had lost his job at Liberty Steel and money got tight. She resented having to share with her little sister. She didn't stop picking on her until the day she left for California.

She pulled out the tape and turned off the television. The house felt even smaller. Chips in the wall reminded her of places she'd pushed Kristyna when they were kids. One of the cushions on the couch had a black stain from when she'd dumped a mixing bowl of hot fudge on her sister's head. Kristyna had to go to school for a week with embarrassing cream on her scalp. Danuta had forgotten all these things. Maybe her sister hadn't.

The pizza arrived. She took it and a can of V8 to her father's study. She needed to send thank you emails to the wives of campaign donors. The pizza had so much salt her throat went dry after two pieces. She polished off the V8 and put her legs on the desk and leaned back in her father's office chair. She checked her Facebook page. The usual people had clicked 'like' on a selfie she snapped before her plane took off that morning. Her friend Anita, a judge from Carmel, had posted a recipe for Hummus peanut butter she'd have to try when she returned. She read gossip on the *TMZ* site. Knowing about the latest sham marriage in Hollywood came in handy at grueling socializers. When she got bored with the gossip, she clicked over to the satellite page. The windows to her parents' bedroom were still dark, but the white smudge had disappeared. She put her legs on the floor and sat straight. Wind howled outside and shook the walls. She moved the image down, tried to zoom closer on the large picture window from the kitchen, then swiveled it until it shifted to a view of the side of the house facing their neighbors.

The smudge appeared in the lower corner of her sister's bedroom window. She closed the pizza box and carried it and the empty V8 can to the kitchen. She put the pizza in the refrigerator. Her sister would probably want it. Looked like she ate that sort of crap every day. She smacked her forehead. "Stop it," she said out loud. Why did the urge to pick on Kristyna surface so easily? Like a disease. She hadn't kept in touch with any outside family since her

Uncle Jarek had come into her room at Christmas, when she was a senior in high school. He'd scooted close to her and put his hand on her knee. "Am I making you nervous?" he'd said. She marched downstairs to tell her mother, who told her she was crazy. Beyond her sister, she had no real family left, just the people she'd inherited when she married Enrique.

The sun bounced off Lake Arthur, turned it into a mirror. She stepped outside the kitchen door and made her way past the dead roses in her mother's garden to the hill leading to the water. As a teenager, she'd sit on the banks reading Tom Robbins novels. It had been a place of peace, solace from her father's constant criticisms. It didn't have the same effect now. The air had gotten colder since the afternoon. She turned around and climbed the hill. The windows to her parents' bedroom looked like black eyes, staring at her. She walked around the other side to check out her and her sister's windows. They were just as dark. No white smudge, no lurking, ghostly face. The pictures from the satellite page must have been flawed. Or maybe the lens on the camera used to take them hadn't been properly cleaned.

The wind spit ice through her bones. Dirty clouds roiled toward Haggard from Chicago and Gary. She hurried back inside.

In her father's study, she opened Word and wrote a generic thank you note she'd send to the wives of donors who'd given her husband enough money to cover his last reelection campaign. She could have whipped it up with her eyes closed, she'd done it so many times. Didn't seem much different from the mindless yip-yap she engaged in at social events. Three hours prep to stand in a reception area with a cup of spiked punch in one hand while she used her other hand to cover her mouth, pretending to be amused by the phony people around her. She wondered if all that robotic behavior had built the wall she'd put between herself and her hometown. Part of her yearned to be young again, to be rolling with the Bacos, the town stoners, hanging out in a bunker near the reservoir, cutting class to go to Chicago and meet rich douchebags who thought imitating Judd Nelson's character in *The Breakfast Club* made them cool. They'd all become stockbrokers and politicians. Like Enrique, the man she'd married because he wore five hundred-dollar cufflinks and had the softest hands she'd ever felt on a man. Nothing like her angry, patriarchal father who'd come home with dirt caked onto his concrete fingers. He'd stand at the kitchen sink, scrubbing them with Goop, complaining they'd never be clean.

She sent the emails and closed the browser. The satellite page waited for her beneath it. The smudge had vanished from her sister's window. She rotated the image several times and stopped when the smudge flashed on the living room window facing the front yard. A groan travelled from the second floor down the stairs and to the dining room. The wind raged and the walls rattled. She stood and slammed the door to the study and locked it. Thunder popped and boomed like fireworks. The lamp overhead blinked, as did the computer. The power failed and the room went dark.

"Shit!" She tried to remember where she'd put her cell phone. She wanted to talk to someone, anyone. Her husband, her sister. As sheets of rain pelted the roof, the wooden floors creaked and moaned like a pack of dogs howling at the moon. She patted down her pockets. Her jeans had been a bit too tight, she remembered. She'd put her phone in her purse, which she'd left in the living room after digging through it to find cash to tip the pizza boy. "Shit!" she said again, louder. Thunder clapped in circles around the house. She peered through the blinds. Black clouds covered the sky like a blanket. Lightning strobed across the horizon. How scared she'd been as a child, anytime a Lake Michigan storm cut loose and threatened northern Indiana. She'd grab her little sister from her bed and tell her to sleep on the floor of her room. In those days, she'd told herself her sister would protect her. Ludicrous! Her sister was four years younger. No, she realized, she'd brought her sister into her room as cannon fodder. Whatever monsters might have climbed down from above, she'd have offered them Kristyna in exchange for her own life. Did her sister even remember? She'd been so young. How she wished she were there right then—she'd apologize to her for all the nasty things she'd done to her when they were growing up.

She spoke to the clouds outside—"I'm sorry." She'd been the worst big sister in the history of big sisters. As if agreeing, the sky rumbled and shook the earth. The window rattled, the blinds chattered, and the handle on the door to the study rocked in jittery turns, as though someone on the other side were testing it. She covered her ears and screamed, "I said I'm sorry!"

An atomic thunderclap sent a shockwave through the house. Danuta crawled under the desk and put her hands over the back of her neck. Despite denouncing religion the moment she arrived in California, all those years ago, despite countless jokes she'd made about "hayseeds" back home who "still believed in all that God crap," she closed her eyes and asked God to make the storm go away. She peered over her shoulder, at the blinds and the window behind them, expecting the sky to clear on her request.

Smeared across the rain-soaked panes, fragmented by the blinds covering them, the smudge she'd seen on the satellite page stared back at her. She groped for the plastic tilt wand on the far side and twirled it until the blinds came together nice and snug. Maybe she'd hallucinated the white, ghostly face, maybe not. No need to take chances.

She fell asleep and dreamt about growing up in Haggard, Indiana. She saw friends, lovers, and family she hadn't considered in decades. When sunlight peeked through the pinholes in the blinds and crows outside cawed like old couples arguing, she rolled out from under the desk. She put her hands on the office chair to support her as she stood. Electricity had been restored. The computer had rebooted itself. She lifted a blind near the spot she'd seen the smudge on the window. Orphan raindrops, and nothing else, decorated the glass. Before heading outside to get her luggage so she could shower and change into her clothes for the funeral, she checked the satellite page, retyping her parent's address. After zooming in to the street-level image of their house, she rotated it several times. The smudge, or face, or whatever her imagination wanted to call it, could not be found.

Her dress had gotten snug. She hadn't worn it since Jerry Francetti's funeral, five years ago. She'd purchased it specifically for the former senator's burial. It had looked sleek and sexy on her. Now it threatened to rip at the seams. "Got to stop eating ice cream on the weekends," she said as she assessed herself in a tall mirror in the upstairs bathroom.

She drank two cans of V8 for breakfast and sent more emails before Kristyna knocked on the front door. When Danuta saw her sister, she almost broke down and cried. In spite of the confused look on her sister's face, she grabbed her and pulled her in for a real hug. She squeezed her shoulders and spoke into her ear—"Jesus Christ," she said, "I hope you can forgive me."

"For what?"

"Stop it."

Her sister gripped her tighter. She sniffled, then bawled. They collapsed onto the crumbling front stoop and held each other until they both needed tissues. Danuta found a travel pack in her purse and offered her sister one before she took one for herself.

They glanced at each other. The smile on her sister's face looked almost as full and confident as the smile she'd worn in the faded picture in their father's study. Her sister honked her nose and crumpled the tissue in her hand. "It's okay," she said. "If I'd had a little sister, I would have picked on her just the same." She poked Danuta in the shoulder, no doubt expecting her to laugh with her.

"No," said Danuta. "You're better than me."

"All right," said her sister, "if you insist." She patted her on the knee and hoisted herself up with the help of the crooked rail. "I apologize for the mess in my car," she said, nodding to the old station wagon parked near the street.

Danuta stood and brushed dirt off the back of her dress. "Screw it," she said. "Let's take mine." She started for the alley along the side of the house before her sister could argue. "From now on," she said as she walked, "you and I are going to set aside a time, each week, to chat on Skype. I won't take no for an answer."

She opened the passenger door and held it for her sister like a chauffer. "My lady," she said as her sister ducked into the car. She helped her fold part of her dress over her knee and shut the door. As she walked around to the driver's side, she paused. She'd only looked at her sister through the passenger window for a moment, but she'd seen it in the glass—the white smudge, obscuring her sister's face, the ghostly image, grinning at Danuta like a rival.

ATOMIC FUEL

Sal Bridgewater sang along to a Nirvana tune on the classic alternative station, assured his empty passenger seat he didn't have a gun. The song gave way to a jingle for an energy drink he'd never heard of—*Be strong as an ox and sharp as a tack, drink Atomic Fuel when laziness attacks!* The melody was hypnotic, like a concession ad at a drive-in movie. When he realized he'd been humming along, he turned down the volume. Despite being a tool for corporate America, he maintained his youthful, if hypocritical, disgust for runaway capitalism. Waking at six in the morning and going to the same cubicle every day seemed worse than death. He'd fallen behind in his paperwork at Agra Insurance. His boss, an insufferable douche named Craig Nash, often said he didn't believe Sal had the enthusiasm required to do a good job.

Be strong as an ox and sharp as a tack...

He shook his head to throw the jingle from his mind. It didn't work. And what were they pushing? An energy drink? He didn't even like coffee. Where did they sell that sort of crap? He scanned the road until he spotted a Family Express convenient store. He pulled into the lot and parked.

The front door rang like a coo-coo clock, alerting a skinny cashier with square glasses that a customer had arrived. The young man had tied a red bandana around his head like Bruce Springsteen. Sal asked if they carried Atomic Fuel. The cashier

21

pointed to coolers along the far wall. "I love it," he said. "Can't stop drinking it."

Sal hurried through an aisle of shelves loaded with potato chips and processed pastries. Yellow florescent lights overhead buzzed like bickering flies. The Atomic Fuel cans were tall and skinny with a mushroom cloud in between labels on the front and the back. He grabbed a couple and returned to the cashier.

He drank the first can as he merged with Lublin's scant, morning rush hour traffic. His heart beat faster. His hands shook on the steering wheel. He pumped his fist to a Pearl Jam song despite his hatred of Pearl Jam. The jingle followed—*Be strong as an ox and sharp as a tack...* He bobbed his head and sang along. He popped the lid on the second can and finished it as he pulled into work. He strutted through the front doors of Agra Insurance with the gait of a man who'd just won the lottery.

Petra Kosobuki, a brunette from Crown Point whose eyeliner made her look like a cat, smiled and said, "Somebody's got some pep in their step!" She'd told him once she wanted to be a police officer. He'd asked why, as though she'd confessed to being a mass murderer. She hadn't spoken to him since. Now, she looked like she'd go anywhere with him if he asked.

George Binder, whose cologne stank up the cubicle next to Sal's, asked him if he'd gotten some action the night before—"You wet your dipstick?" He sat in his rolling chair rigid as a corpse and uttered the crass question like a pundit on a boring, PBS roundtable. Sal's boss had once told him to look to George for an example of what he called "high energy performance."

Firing up his computer and sitting down, Sal said, "No such luck."

George frowned. "Normally, you still look asleep in the morning." He slapped him on the back and laughed. "And you don't look too much different when you leave in the afternoon!"

"Thanks, George." He took the first case off the stack of folders on his desk. Ms. Lilly Willet. Full coverage. Rear-ended by a Porsche on I-65. The driver had been zooming from Chicago to Miami. He'd swerved onto the median to pass traffic in the far-left lane. A bulldozer swung out from a construction site, forcing the idiot to squeeze back onto the road. He couldn't slow down and he couldn't quite fit between Ms. Willet's station wagon and the car behind her. The Porsche crumpled like an aluminum can. The driver had Advantage insurance and they demanded Agra replace the Porsche. Sal had wanted to fight them, but Craig insisted the company would lose a suit brought on by Advantage. So now he had to explain to Ms. Willet, sixty-six years old, choir director at St. Bridget's in Haggard, why her premiums were going to increase. Jesus, he hated this job.

Be strong as an ox...

Craig Austin waddled through the aisles greeting employees. He'd worn his usual—a pink and white-striped button-down shirt and brown slacks. He'd swept his thinning blond hair across the top of his head. He spoke like Mickey Mouse. Normally, he'd offer Sal a flippant, diplomatic "Good morning." He stopped, however, and said, "Bridgewater? You already working a case?"

Sal said, "Trying to get up to speed." He couldn't sit still. Craig's high, annoying voice grated his spine like the screech of a dentist's drill. He wanted to grab his computer monitor and smash it into his face.

Putting his hands on Sal's shoulders and giving them a squeeze, Craig said, "By God, we may make you an insurance man yet, yes we may."

What a horrible fate. Sal pictured himself in twenty years—middle-aged, overweight, probably married and divorced three times, still sitting in a cubicle eight hours a day, cheating policy holders.

and sharp as a tack...

He blurted out, "It's Atomic Fuel, sir."

Craig curled his lips. "Yes?" He sounded phony patient, like a parent humoring a child.

Sal stood. "I discovered it this morning. Atomic Fuel, that is. It's the reason I'm ready to work my tail off."

His boss lightened up. "Well," he said, "whatever it takes." He tried to swing around the end of the aisle.

"You ever try it?" said Sal.

"Excuse me?"

Sal sang the jingle—"*Be strong as an ox and sharp as a tack, drink Atomic Fuel when laziness attacks!*" He put his hands out when he finished, expecting applause.

Craig nodded and said, "I'll have to give it a day in court."

"Promise?"

His boss hop-stepped to the next row of cubicles.

Sal sat back down. He put on his headset and punched Ms. Willet's phone number into the computer. As he listened to the woman's line ring on the other end, he hummed the jingle. He should have bought more cans of Atomic Fuel. Not just for himself, but for his coworkers. People needed to *know*.

"Hello?" Ms. Willet had a pleasant voice. She reminded him of every school teacher who'd ever been kind to him. All two or three of them.

He explained the situation to her, apologized on behalf of Agra Insurance. Then he got to the part he despised. "Ms. Willet, for your troubles, we'd like to help you out with your medical expenses. We're willing to pay fifteen percent and…" He cleared his throat. "Ms. Willet, can we discuss something else for a moment?"

She said sure, go ahead. "Sounds like I'm screwed no matter what you tell me."

"Ms. Willet," he said, "have you ever heard of Atomic Fuel?"

"What?" Now she reminded him of his other teachers from school—angry, bitter, and impatient.

"It's an energy drink," he said. "Perhaps you've heard the commercial on the radio." And then he sang it for her.

Before he finished, she cut in—"Mr. Bridgewater, I know you're trying to butter me up for this royal screw-job, but I certainly don't need to listen to you pitch some garbage soft drink. It's bad enough…"

"Garbage? Ms. Willet, it's hardly fair to judge a product before you've tried it."

"You know what?" she said. "I need to speak with your supervisor."

Sal's head cleared for a moment. "I apologize," he said. "I apologize profusely."

"That's well and good," she said, "but I still want to speak to, who's running that office, Annie Crowell?"

"No ma'am," he said. "Just a minute." He should have been nervous about the lecture he'd receive from Craig. But if his boss called him to his office to chew him out, he'd have another opportunity to tell him about Atomic Fuel.

He found a different file to work on in the meantime—The Shipwick Case. Mrs. Shipwick had died in a car accident four years ago. Mr. Shipwick had fought the company ever since to receive his wife's due compensation. He'd been murdered in his house for a bunk lottery ticket a few months back. His son, Dan, had taken up the cause of collecting on his mother's insurance. Sal's job, each and every time the folder wove its way back to his desk, was to convince the family not to sue. He reached the son on the phone. "Mr. Shipwick," he said, "Sal Bridgewater, Agra Insurance. Got a moment?"

"My lawyer says not to talk to you guys."

"Oh, Mr. Shipwick, you retained an attorney?"

"What do you think?"

"Well now," said Sal, "we went over this last February, remember? I told you the cost of hiring a lawyer versus the best possible outcome for you in a lawsuit…it just doesn't add up. You're probably starting to see that now. How much does your lawyer charge? Two-fifty, three, four-hundred an hour?"

"That's none of your business," said Dan Shipwick. "You guys are grifters, you understand? You're con artists. You should be put out of business."

Sal grabbed the bridge of his nose and squeezed. A headache, in its infancy, crawled along the top of his skull.

when laziness attacks…

"Mr. Shipwick?" he said. "Have you ever tried Atomic Fuel?"

The man on the other end said nothing.

"Surely you've caught the commercial on the radio." He sang it for him, in case he hadn't.

Dan Shipwick hung up.

Sal rummaged through his files for another case. He really needed to take a break, head to the nearest convenience store, and get another can or two of Atomic Fuel. He stood and put on his jacket.

George Binder, having just finished a call, looked over and said, "Got to drain the weasel?"

"Just going to take a trip to the Family Express on Temple Avenue."

Craig Austin burst from his office, nearly slamming his door into the wall. "Bridgewater!" he said.

Crap. "Yes sir," said Sal. Jesus, he never called his boss 'sir.' Probably another positive by-product of Atomic Fuel. He pushed his chair in and marched down to his boss's office.

Craig had already taken a seat behind his desk. He squeezed a stress toy painted like a baseball in his right hand. He directed Sal to the smaller, uncomfortable chair across from him. "You know why you're here, don't you?" He sounded like a father who'd grown tired of disciplining the same child for the same infraction.

Sal rubbed his sweaty, nervous hands back and forth on his knees. "I think so."

"Good, that's good." Craig leaned forward and put the stress ball in a brass bowl next to a row of Baltimore Orioles bobble-heads. "You tell me what you think Ms. Willet just said on the phone."

The shades on the window were slit. Sunlight snuck in and splashed framed pictures of Oriole Park on the walls in blinding white glares. Sal knew the boss wanted an apology for his treatment of Ms. Willet. Instead, he said, "She didn't understand the benefits."

"She's not supposed to," said Craig. "Policies are written so only lawyers can understand them."

"Atomic Fuel, sir," said Sal. "She didn't understand the benefits of Atomic Fuel."

His boss slapped himself in the forehead. "What is wrong with you?"

"I've been enlightened, sir."

Craig stood and paced between his desk and an umbrella holder filled with signed baseball bats. "Let's play on an even field here, Bridgewater."

"Good idea."

The boss's pants whooshed as he sat on the edge of his desk. "I really don't like you. And you know that."

"I've always assumed it."

"Somehow, you survived the training period, managed to keep your job here." The more honest he got, the higher his voice sailed. "I've been looking for an excuse to can you or send you to the Haggard office. I just, gosh, I just don't like you, Bridgewater. Something about you, I don't know what. Normally, you're like a slug, and that gets right under my skin, seeing someone drag their feet around the office, acting like they'd rather be someplace else. And now..." He laughed and looked at the ceiling. "Now you're acting like a dope fiend."

"Not dope, sir," said Sal. "Atomic Fuel. It's legal."

Craig made his way back to the plush, leather chair behind his desk. "I want you to go to your cubicle, sit down, work your cases without any more complaints or, so help me..."

"Yes, sir." Sal started for the door. "I'm just going to run to the Family Express for some more Atomic Fuel."

Craig slammed his fist onto his desk and stood. His voice scaled dog-whistle frequencies. "Are you out of your mind?"

Sal's blood calmed, his confidence surged. "Mr. Austin," he said, "I've done nothing wrong here. I've found something good and I'm getting persecuted for sharing it."

"You know what?" Craig walked around his desk and pointed to the parking lot. "Take the rest of the day off."

"I don't need to..."

The boss's jowls puffed, like the slightest pinprick would make his head explode. "Bridgewater!"

Sal put his hand out. "Relax, sir. If you'd like a can of Atomic Fuel, I'll buy you one. My treat."

"Get out!"

Refusing to leave, Sal shut the door and stared down his boss. "Now you listen to me..." He poked Craig in his chest as he spoke. "I will not stand by and allow you to badmouth this drink, act like it's not something special."

The boss's complexion paled. In a quiet, humble tone, he said, "Do I need to call the police?"

How could his boss be so narrow-minded? Sal shoved him out of the way and grabbed a Louisville Slugger from the umbrella can. "What kind of Indiana man roots for the Orioles?"

"Put that down." Craig's hand shook as he pointed at the baseball bat.

"Let me show you just how much energy I have." Sal swiped the bobble-heads with one swing, sent them flying into the wall. They shattered like dishes. Fragments landed in flower patterns on the carpet. He said, "Watch me cut this in two." Then he beat the top of the desk. The bat splintered. He gave up on the desk and bashed the glass covering the pictures of Oriole Stadium on the wall.

Craig shouted to Petra Kosobuki, "Call the cops! Now!"

Sal dropped the bat. "No need for all that." He shoved him out of his way and headed for the front door. His co-workers stood, silent and stupid, as though Big Foot were stomping through the office. Before he left, he said, "Anyone need anything from the Family Express?"

Nobody answered.

He hurried up Temple Avenue to the convenient store. Wouldn't be long before the energy drinks from that morning wore off. Police sirens wailed nearby. The young woman behind the counter at the Family Express held a *Cosmo* magazine in front of her face. Her teeth chattered. She looked at Sal and smirked. She tossed a lock of her purple hair away from her eyes.

Sal grabbed an entire six-pack of Atomic Fuel. The young lady placed her magazine on a display case filled with donuts. She nodded at the drinks and said, "That's good stuff, ain't it?"

"You know it," said Sal.

As she rung him up, a Lublin squad car, lights flashing without the siren, pulled in front of the door at an angle. A hefty officer squeezed out of the driver's side and entered the store.

Sal took his change from the girl and wedged the six-pack of Atomic Fuel under his arm. "Afternoon," he said to the cop.

"Not quite." The officer rested his palm on his nightstick. "You Sal Bridgewater?"

"Yes I am."

"You going to give me a hassle?"

"No, sir."

"Very good." The cop told him to stay where he was. He examined the pastries in the donut display case. "Wrap a lemon twister for me, honey, why don't you?" he said to the cashier.

She put the pastry in a bag and handed it to him. "No charge." She looked at Sal as though he'd thrown up on her.

The cop tapped Sal's shoulder with the bag. "Let's go, buddy." He told him to stand by the trunk of the squad car.

Sal said, "You mind if I have one of my drinks?"

"Go ahead." The cop talked into the handset on his shoulder, told his dispatch he had the suspect. He requested support and a paddy wagon. Then he broke into the bag with the pastry and started munching. "We're going to hang here for a moment, you don't mind."

"Sure thing." Sal asked if he had a regular radio in the car.

"Yup." The cop pounded his chest. Had a chunk of the lemon twister gotten lodged near his heart?

Sal offered him a can of Atomic Fuel.

"What is it?" said the cop.

"A life-changer." He passed him a can.

The cop stared at it for a moment, then opened it and took a sip. "Tastes great," he said.

"Doesn't it?" Sal asked him to tune the radio in the car to the classic alternative station.

"I hate that crap." After another drink of Atomic Fuel, the cop said, "Well, whatever." He opened the passenger-side door, leaned in, and turned on the car's normal radio. He dialed until he came to a Soundgarden song. "This must be it."

Sal agreed.

"You know," said the cop, holding up his can of Atomic Fuel, turning it in his hand, "I can already feel this stuff working."

Sal asked if he wanted another.

"Why not?" The cop finished his second can in one noisy guzzle. The jingle came on the radio.

"This is it." Sal told him to keep quiet for a moment.

Be strong as an ox...

When the commercial ended, Sal said, "Can you believe my boss called you guys just because I wanted to share this with them? With the policyholders? With the *world?*"

The officer shook his head. "Damn shame, I tell you."

"It's not too late," said Sal.

The officer grinned. He ducked into the car and pulled a shotgun from a thin locker mounted on the roof between the front and back seats. "Maybe folks don't want to listen to you," he said. "They *have* to listen to me."

"Now you're talking," said Sal.

SIDEWALK FLOWERS

Every morning, Helen Bobble emerged from her house and slowly
made her way to her front walk. She proceeded to wash leaves and
other debris off the stretch of concrete between her lawn and the
street with a garden hose.

The kids arrived halfway through the task. John Barker, Andy
Bumble, and Kelly Bobo. Chocolate smeared around their mouths
like mud.

"What you doing, Ms. Bobble?"

Helen ignored their taunts.

"Growing sidewalk flowers?"

The children's faces and names altered. Their insults did not.
In her seventies, she'd argue, "Can't think of anything original to
say?" Now, in her pragmatic eighties, she let them prattle on, like
broken records, saying the same thing every day.

Then Andy Bumble said something she hadn't heard before:

"Why are you too lazy to use a broom?"

Helen stopped, looked at her frail body, her tiny arms. Long
after her friends had been placed in retirement homes, long after
everyone she knew throughout her life had passed away, she still
had the strength to take care of herself. How could this little brat
not see that?

"You should be ashamed of yourself," she said.

Andy stuck out his tongue at her.

She picked up the hose and showered all three of the children with water. They screamed and scattered, coming together once more across the street.

"I'm telling my mom!" said John Barker.

Helen smiled and continued watering her sidewalk.

The children decided old Ms. Bobble needed to be taught a lesson. They took turns making number two in a brown paper bag. They rolled it up and stole a lighter from John's father.

As soon as their parents went to sleep, they snuck out and met across the street from Ms. Bobble's house. The only lights came from lamps lining the sides of the road. They crept across it, opened Ms. Bobble's creaky gate, and slipped inside her yard.

They failed to notice a rumbling rising from the sidewalk.

Andy placed the bag at Ms. Bobble's door. John got the lighter going, held it to the bag. As soon as it caught fire, Kelly rang the bell. As they ran toward the sidewalk, the patch of concrete Ms. Bobble watered every morning opened, like a giant mouth.

Kelly and John hurtled the gap. They sped for their homes without looking back. By the time Andy got there, a concrete claw had formed. As he leapt, the claw grabbed him.

He screamed.

Ms. Bobble's front door opened, and the old woman poked her head out.

Andy waved to her, cried her name.

Ms. Bobble's eyes glowed from the flames bouncing off the burning bag on her porch. She made no effort to help the child being devoured by her sidewalk or even extinguish the fire before her.

The next morning, Kelly and John went to inquire about their friend Andy. They turned away as soon as they saw two police cars in the Bumble driveway. "She probably caught him and turned him in," Kelly said.

They decided to make their morning rounds, beginning with testing Ms. Bobble while she watered her sidewalk.

"What you doing, Ms. Bobble?"

The old woman wore a tiny smile.

"Growing sidewalk flowers?"

Ms. Bobble chuckled. The water from her hose turned light red as it brushed debris into the grass and dirt.

CANOPY ROAD

October, 1981

Henry and Adam had been discussing comic books and their teacher, Mrs. Newsome, who never wore a bra. Her breasts bounced under her sweaters and dresses and her nipples poked out, as though admonishing the boys for staring. Matthew didn't seem as interested as Henry and Adam were, however. He changed the subject any time they talked about their teacher's "cosmic boobs."

They were on Canopy Road, which connected southern portions of town with a wooden, wobbly bridge, allowing the boys to cross Pawpaw Creek from their parents' homes to Oak Crest where, all kids agreed, a vile place such as a school *should* be. Riley Elementary, in fact, sat across the street from Resting Souls cemetery. Any time Mrs. Newsome's lectures about the importance of spelling or cursive writing threatened to put Henry to sleep, he'd gaze out the window at ancient tombstones jutting like crooked teeth from uneven ground in the graveyard. He'd imagine the town's forefathers clawing their way to the surface, decayed and hungry for the flesh of the living.

He and Adam had started an argument over who they'd rather hang out with—Elektra or Catwoman. Adam asked for one good reason why Henry thought he was "too good" for Elektra. Henry said, "Because girls shouldn't be tougher than me. My father told me that, you ask him." Matthew called him old fashioned, said modern women could whip any guy they wanted. He stopped and counted the books in his hand.

"Crap," he said. "I think I dropped my handwriting folder." He glanced backward, as though he might spot it on the road behind him. Then he looked up and shrieked. He pointed toward the sky.

Yellow and brown leaves rustled overhead as a large animal leapt from tree to tree.

Henry and Adam raced for the bridge across Pawpaw Creek. Matthew waddled like a penguin and screamed. Henry slowed down, nearly slipped on fallen leaves slicked by a recent rain. He grabbed Matthew by the shoulder and urged him to move faster. Branches snapped and twigs tumbled to the ground. Matthew found the speed to pass both Henry and Adam.

They stomped across the wooden bridge loud enough to wake angry spirits rumored to lurk near the water. The trees on Canopy Road gave way to lawns and residential neighborhoods. Whatever Matthew had seen had given up the chase and returned to the shade and shelter of Oak Crest.

Outside of Henry's dad's house, they slowed and caught their breath. Matthew dropped to the sidewalk, letting his books scatter. Henry and Adam rested their hands on their knees. Once able to speak, Henry said, "What the...?"

Adam shook his head. "I'm not sure I saw anything."

Matthew said, "I certainly did." He picked leaves from the bottoms of his shoes. "Like a white monkey," he said, "swinging, swinging, just like a monkey." He said the beast had the foul face of a possum—a rough snout and black, lifeless eyes. "I saw its claws," he said. "Sharp as butcher knives, sharp as the fangs in its mouth."

Henry looked at Adam. Matthew was prone to inventing stories. His mother passed the habit to him, having generated a reputation as a gossip. His father, a truck driver, never seemed to be home, never seemed to be around to set him straight.

"I don't know," said Adam. "You want grownups looking at us funny, the way they look at crazy Mr. Larsen?"

Henry said, "Maybe we should just take the bus."

"No." Adam slammed his foot on the concrete. "No way I'm riding with second and third graders."

"Well," said Matthew, "if it wanted to attack us, it would have."
Henry and Adam waited for more.

"Just seems to me," he said, "if we travel together, we'll be safe."

Adam snapped his fingers. He hooked his thumbs in the straps on his backpack. "Matthew knows what's up. He makes straight A's. We walk together, we'll be okay."

Matthew agreed, though he didn't look convinced.

The conversation shifted to more important issues, such as whose parents would drive them to the mall in Merrillville to see *Time Bandits* and whether Mrs. Newsome would get fired for not wearing a bra. Henry couldn't decide. "She's called home twice just because I don't write pretty cursive," he said. But he loved staring at her boobs and worried her replacement might not dress so casual.

Adam and Matthew moved on to their homes. Henry went inside his father's house hoping the old man would still be asleep.

As he snuck into the front hall, he set his backpack carefully, quietly, on the hardwood floor. The steps leading upstairs creaked and his dad clomped down in his boxers, a stained t-shirt, and a pink robe that had belonged to Henry's mother. He carried a half-empty glass of whiskey. "Hey, buddy." He tried to smile. Henry hadn't seen his father produce a genuine smile since before his mother died. His father had insisted she drive him to work during a blizzard. On her way back, a snowplow ran her into a tree. "Why you sweating?" said his father.

Henry shrugged. "Guess I'm hot."

His father looked past him, at the slender windows on either side of the front door. "Looks like it's forty degrees out there." He grabbed him by his hair and yanked him closer. "You going to tell me the truth?"

Henry fought the urge to cry. That would really make the old man angry. "We were running," he said.

"Racing, or what?"

"There might be a monster in the trees, on Canopy Road."

His father said, "Excuse me?"

He tried describing the creature as Matthew had. He couldn't remember all the details.

His father slapped him in the mouth and said, "Insult my intelligence again, son. See what happens."

The next day, Henry and Adam took the long way home. He assured Adam he had no fear of Canopy Road. "It's just," he said, "you know, we should check out Henneker's, see if they got anything new on the rack."

Adam said it would be stupid for just the two of them to travel Canopy Road.

Matthew had been held after school by Mrs. Newsome. She'd caught him drawing Conan the Barbarian while the rest of the class had been writing sentences using the week's spelling words. She'd taken his picture and shredded it with her sharp, painted nails. When Matthew cried, she told him to stand in the corner. He blurted some nonsense about how he didn't find her punishments "civil," or "human," so she said they could discuss her classroom management techniques in private. None of that made sense to Henry and when he asked Adam about it, Adam called it "smart people gibberish."

They took the north bridge across Pawpaw Creek and ducked into Henneker's, a drug store that still had a soda fountain and ten-cent Coca-Cola bottles. It occupied the first floor of a two-story brown brick building their grandparents said once housed a secret society of wealthy cannibals. No new comics had been placed on the turning rack.

Outside, crazy Mr. Larsen sat on a crumbling, stone bench, sketching odd symbols, like hieroglyphics, in the dirt between the sidewalk and the road, using a rusted hunting knife. The adults told them to stay away from him. They called him "sick," though they wouldn't explain how or why. When he saw Henry and Adam, the pupils of his eyes grew big and black. "Gentlemen," he said. He had to be at least a hundred years old. His yellow skin had wrinkled so much he resembled ancient oaks near the cemetery. Most of his teeth were missing, making him ghoulish, like ancestors the grownups spoke of in hushed tones.

"Back off," said Adam. He kicked the knife from Mr. Larsen's shaking hands and used his shoe to rub out the symbols he'd scratched in the dirt. "My dad catches you yapping at us," he said, "he'll clobber you something good."

The crazy man grinned, showed his awful teeth. When he spoke, a rotting stench soured the air. "Oh, the things I know about your father!"

"Let's go." Adam tugged on Henry's shirt and dragged him toward Harvest Avenue, which connected with Canopy Road on the residential side of the bridge.

Henry's father woke him after midnight. He stood in the doorway of his bedroom, dressed in his security guard uniform. He shone his flashlight back and forth in the darkness. "Wake up, buddy," he said.

As Henry changed from his gray and yellow Batman pajamas into the clothes he'd worn to school that day, he understood something terrible had happened. His father complained about how much he had to work to pay property taxes on the house. He'd go to his job at the cemetery with a hundred and three-degree fever. He never came home early, and he never took a day off. "What's going on?" he said to his father.

His father told him to hush and hurry downstairs. They got in the Ford truck inherited from Henry's grandfather and rumbled across Harvest Avenue toward downtown. When they passed Henneker's, Henry looked for Mr. Larsen, who supposedly slept in the alley between the drug store and the library. He saw only rats, jumping in and out of a dumpster.

"How did Mr. Larsen get sick?" said Henry.

"He asked too many questions." His father turned up the radio, feigned interest in the early morning farm reports.

At the police station, Adam and his parents, Paul and Judy, sat on a wooden bench, much like the wooden benches in the principal's office at Riley Elementary. His mother rubbed her elbows, as though she were cold, or maybe nervous.

"Have a seat," said his father. He stood near Adam's dad and they talked quietly.

Something unpleasant dragged from Henry's throat to his belly. He wanted to throw up. He leaned against the large back on the bench and waited for someone to tell him anything useful.

The door to the rooms behind the front desk opened. Matthew's mom and dad, Pam and Jonah, were accompanied by Officer Smyth. Officer Smyth had thick eyebrows that had earned him the nickname Caterpillar among the kids in town. He gave a boring talk every year at school about drugs and communists. Matthew's mom, dressed in a green sweater with white reindeer on it, as though Halloween and Thanksgiving had already passed, had turned a cloth handkerchief into a sopping mess. Matthew's dad, bigger and meaner than Henry's father, wore a grim expression. Henry doubted even a chisel and Thor's hammer could remove it. Officer Welker, whom the kids called Boing-Boing because he could stretch a rubber band between his fingers and make actual music, emerged from the back and said to Henry and Adam's parents, "Let's bring the boys in."

They were led to a dim room with a table in the middle, surrounded by wooden chairs. A mirror covered half the far wall. Officer Welker instructed the boys to have a seat. He sat on the opposite side and said, "Matthew told his parents someone chased you yesterday on Canopy Road."

"Not someone," said Henry. "Some*thing*."

The officer looked at him, then at the parents, who'd huddled near the door.

"Yes," said Officer Welker. "I understand he described it as a monster, or some sort of creature, but we know it was a person. In fact, we know who he is, we just need you to point at him so we can arrest him and he won't hurt any more children."

Henry turned to his father. "What's going on?"

"Do what you're told," said his father.

"Okay," said Officer Welker. "We're going to show you some people, and we want you to point to the man who chased you yesterday."

"This is nuts," said Henry.

His father clenched his fists and said, "So help me..."

The officer explained the lights would be turned out and the mirror would become a window. "You're going to see some men on the other side. Point to the bad one."

Henry wondered if the police had caught the creature, and the creature would stand among the other suspects. That would sure show his father. But the mirror changed to a dark glass and five normal, human men stood under a bright lamp, their backs against a height-chart. The first two were Officers Hughes and Smith, who ran a baseball camp in the summer. They'd been dressed in trench coats, t-shirts, and dirty jeans. In the center, Mr. Larsen stared into space, his entire body shaking. On the other side, two more cops, Officers Dixon and Covert, who helped collect presents at the town's annual Christmas drive for the poor, had also been disguised in shabby clothes.

Had his mother been there, Henry would have pointed to one of the cops. She'd encouraged him to speak up in crooked moments. He knew the adults wanted him to say creaky, crumbling Mr. Larsen had somehow whisked through the trees like an orangutan. He decided to do neither.

"Nope," he said.

"How's that?" said Officer Welker.

"None of those guys chased us."

Adam looked relieved for a moment, like maybe that would be it. Henry's refusal to cooperate would put a stop to this nonsense and they'd finally be told what had happened to Matthew.

Officer Welker tapped the table in front of Adam. "How about you?"

Adam turned to his dad.

"How about it?" His dad's navy and gold 4H windbreaker ruffled as he motioned with his hands for his son to hurry up.

Adam had never complained of either of his parents hitting him. Surely, he had nothing to fear by telling the truth. But he bowed his head and, while staring at the table, wagged a finger at Mr. Larsen. "That guy," he said.

Officer Welker said, "Which one, Adam? Can you tell me for sure?"

"Mr. Larsen," he said. "Mr. Larsen bugs us all the time. It was probably him."

"Well now," said Officer Welker, "we need to be sure. We don't want to put an innocent man on trial. Not around here, we don't."

Nodding like a bobble-head doll, Adam said, "I'm sure."

Turning his attention to Henry, Officer Welker said, "That leaves you, Hank."

"Nobody calls me Hank."

His father shot across the room and smacked him in the back of his head with his security guard cap.

Officer Welker positioned himself between them. He waited for Henry's father to sink back into the corner with Adam's parents. Then he said to Henry, "There's no such thing as monsters. Not anymore." He leaned on the table and encouraged Henry to examine the lineup once more. "Now tell me," he said, "which one of those men doesn't look right."

Henry considered folding. He thought about how many times he or Adam or Matthew had reminded Mr. Larsen not to talk to them. How frightened the adults seemed any time a child told them Mr. Larsen had bothered them near the drug store. But the guy was decrepit, falling apart. He could barely lift the hunting knife he used to draw his strange symbols in the dirt. How in the world could he be a threat to anyone, especially someone in the fourth grade? He shook his head, spoke with confidence:

"Nobody human chased us yesterday." He raised his chin toward his father. "And I don't care if you believe me or not."

Officer Welker sighed. He scratched the top of his thinning hair. "Well folks," he said to the adults, "looks like we can't lock him up."

Henry's father resembled a cartoon character on the verge of shooting smoke from his ears.

Adam's dad said, "Henry, what's the matter with you?"

He didn't respond.

"In the meantime," said Adam's mother, blinking too fast and acting as though someone had physically hurt her, "Matthew's killer just gets to walk?"

Henry and Adam looked at each other. The idea refused to settle in Henry's mind. Adults died all the time. Nothing special. But kids? That didn't even happen in the movies.

Adam's parents had suggested the boys go to school with the second and third graders on the bus. Henry's father said he'd think about it.

As Henry poured himself a bowl of Cheerios the next morning, dumping sugar and milk on the cereal, his father sat in the breakfast nook with a bottle of Jim Beam and a couple of sleeping pills. He said, "Make sure you bundle up today. Cold out there." He tossed the drugs into his mouth and chased them with a swig of whiskey.

"Bus'll be heated," said Henry.

"You're not taking the bus."

He stopped pushing the Cheerios under the milk to make them soggy. "But," he said, "walking to school...Matthew..."

His father guzzled more booze and capped the bottle. He slammed it on the wooden table in the breakfast nook. "Matthew's dead because he was a Nancy, you understand?"

Henry said no, he had no idea what that meant.

"The boy was weak," his father said. "My son's a real man. He can handle himself."

Why did his father speak as though he weren't even in the room? "Whatever got Matthew," said Henry, "it's still out there."

"More talk of monsters?" His father removed the utility belt on his uniform. The company he worked for didn't believe in guns. They'd given him mace and a nightstick to fight off any trouble in the graveyard. He took the weapons out so all he had left was a slick strap of leather. He looped it and snapped it. "Dammit boy," he said, "you going to make me whip you when I'm trying to wind down?" He wore a pleading expression, as though he'd been begged by someone else to beat his son. He trudged by him. He stopped and considered him once more. "I think I'd better head out with you."

For a moment, Henry relaxed. His father would do what other dads might do—he'd travel right next to him across Canopy Road. And, by God, if the thing in the trees tried anything, his father would whoop it.

His father sat back down and turned on a small, old-fashioned television set. He found a morning news show and adjusted the antenna until the woman explaining the weather map stopped breaking into white fuzz.

Henry tried to eat his breakfast. The newscast cut to what they called their "Top Story." A man in a beige suit and tie said police had found the body of Matthew Finlay in a pile of leaves along Canopy Road, near Pawpaw Creek. Police claimed they had a suspect, though no arrest had been made. Next to the newscaster, Matthew's third grade yearbook picture floated, like a ghost.

Now it was true. The TV had said so. Henry felt like someone had placed a giant rock inside his stomach and no food would ever be welcome again. He dumped his cereal into the sink.

"What do you think you're doing?" said his father.

He couldn't answer.

His father nodded toward the fridge. "Save it for later," he said. "You think I got money coming out my ears?"

Henry finished dressing in the front hallway, wrapping a scarf around his face and pulling on his gloves. He tried to slip away before his father could tear himself from the television and follow him. When he opened the door, his father said, "Hold on, buddy."

His father moved like a zombie, angling his feet into his wing-tipped shoes. "All right," he said.

They walked down Canopy Road together. Henry felt awkward, unable to figure out why he and his old man couldn't find anything to talk about; his dad liked baseball and he rooted for the Green Bay Packers despite everyone else in Pawpaw Grove pulling for the Bears. He thought comic books were dumb and he hated movies. Maybe he'd be interested in hearing about Mrs. Newsome and how she never wore a bra. Or maybe, like the topic of monsters, that too would earn Henry a smack in the mouth.

He turned right at Harvest Avenue, hoping his dad wouldn't notice him taking the long way. His dad grabbed the hood on his coat. "You think I'm stupid?" He interrupted before he could answer. "You're going to be late." He shoved him toward the bridge across Pawpaw Creek.

The trees on the other side swayed like dancing skeletons. The remaining leaves on the branches flapped like tiny hands, applauding. Crows bickered with the wind. Henry tried one last time to tell his father how scared he was.

"You dilly-dally anymore," said his father, "I'll give you something to worry about."

Henry turned around and walked, shoulders hunched, as fast as he could. The trees blocked the sun. Branches shifted and crackled. A hoarse breeze twisted through them. Dry leaves crunched under his feet. The stone in his belly had been replaced by sharp pains, as though someone were slashing his insides with a butcher's knife.

All noise surrendered to a long, swooshing sound, louder than everything else. Before he spotted it with his eyes, he could hear it, swinging from one tree to another. Its claws sliced into the thicker branches and made a popping sound whenever the creature wedged them out and leapt to the next tree.

Looking back for his father, he saw the old man had gone home. The distance to Riley Elementary and the distance to the bridge over Pawpaw Creek were the same. The mad rustling above increased. He decided to trust Mrs. Newsome, instead of his father. He grabbed the straps on his backpack, squeezed them, and bolted for the school. The ruckus in the trees got louder and the creature produced a high-pitched howl. The crows scattered.

A white blur flew over him and dropped lower and lower in the branches. He could see where the beast would try to cut him off. If he booked as fast as he could, he might beat it. He'd coax it into chasing him right up to the school. Then everybody would see. They'd tell his father he wasn't a liar. And maybe, just maybe, his father would listen.

EMUQ

Ariel instructed Bernard on where to relocate the self-help section in the bookstore. He barely heard her. His boss had worn a low-cut, frizzy sweater. Her skin smelled like coconut and her long, tan skirt hugged her hips, revealing the outline of her panties. She said, "Are you listening?"

"Yeah, sure." He would have preferred working near the religion shelves. Any time Ariel rang out a customer or disappeared in the break room to strip paperbacks for return, he'd sneak a peak at one of the esoteric volumes mixed in with the Bibles and Korans.

He must have been gawking at her. She blushed and said, "What are you waiting for?"

Before Bernard could load books onto a dolly and cart them across the store, Lucky Camona walked in, dressed in his usual dark slacks and button-down shirt. Despite being indoors, he refused, as always, to remove his thick sunglasses. Folks in Lublin put him in his late 80s. No one knew for sure. He'd moved to America from Egypt many years ago. He spent most of his time at Houck's Deli flirting with women one-third his age. He belonged to enough fraternal organizations to fill his nights with meetings at various lodges around Lake County.

And Bernard loved talking with him. Lucky told stories of his father's amazing misfortunes during both World Wars. He spoke of unnamable creatures he'd encountered across Europe, Africa, and Asia.

As Ariel watched the old man take his trademark tiny steps, his back hunched and his head swiveling like a dinosaur, she smirked. "You get ten minutes with the nuisance," she said to Bernard. "He doesn't buy anything, send him on his way."

Lucky approached the religion section.

Bernard caught up with him. "Doubt we've gotten anything new since last week."

They perused the lone shelf of books about languages long dead, alchemy, cryptozoology, and other belief systems mocked by the cynical masses. "This is really basic stuff," said Lucky. "You should have been around when Seth Crowell had his shop down in Indy." He shook his head and made a tisk-tisk noise. "Those were the days, my young friend."

Bernard had read online how Seth Crowell had cast a Magick spell to neuter one of his daughter's suitors. The price he paid for his jealousy had been severe—witnesses claimed to have seen him and his daughter abducted by humanoid beasts with scaly, olive-green skin and black eyes no bigger than pepper grains.

"You ever buy anything there?" said Bernard.

Lucky turned to him. He was thin, wrinkled, as one would expect a man his age to be, but he was also tall, and when he stared down at him, his stature trumped the plagues of time and gravity. "That's where I found and purchased the book *Emuq*."

Bernard didn't want to admit he'd never heard of it.

Lucky grinned. "It's not the sort of thing one learns about in Indiana."

Bernard's blood raced the way it did anytime his boss Ariel swayed by, showering him with her natural and unnatural scents, or tossed her shaded, bobbed hair and laughed at his concerns about MK-Ultra and Project Paperclip. He tapped his foot, as though his interest in *Emuq* would drain from his shoes.

"It originated in Macedonia," said Lucky. "It may be opened only by candlelight in otherwise pure darkness. It is to be read aloud. As you absorb its knowledge, demons tear at your soul to keep you from unlocking its power. Should you survive the ordeal, you will be gifted with the ability to heal the pain of others."

"Really?" He said it as though he didn't believe the old man.

Then he reprimanded himself. Skepticism cursed the weak, clueless, manipulated masses.

Lucky said, "The book is written in blood. Shall I tell you whose?"

Bernard nodded like a pubescent boy offered a peek at a beautiful woman undressing.

"You must employ this gift in the service of others, not yourself. This is the mistake many men have made over the centuries. Should you use it, in any way, for your own benefit, those same demons will return and drag you to oblivion and drain your blood to ink the next edition of *Emuq* set loose upon the Earth."

Bernard thought of his parents. They would have laughed at someone like Lucky Camona. They'd raised Bernard to be a good, obedient atheist. And they'd failed. His grandfather, a devout Catholic, had given him a comic book version of The Bible when he was still young and his imagination granted the universe tremendous secrets. He'd been on a search for forbidden knowledge ever since. "How can you be sure it works?"

Lucky told him about a man he'd known in Egypt named Ammon. Ammon had read an edition of *Emuq* he'd purchased in Morocco. He'd emerged from a cave certain he had the power to heal any pain. "Like all who have dared to open this book," said Lucky, "he swore he would put his abilities to altruistic use. This changed, however, when his habit of smoking two packs of unfiltered Gitanes a day infected his lungs. While in a cancer ward, he put his hands on his chest and vanquished his own suffering." According to Lucky, shadows swept across the hospital and obliterated Ammon. "Not one week later," said Lucky, "a Masonic brother of mine found a copy of *Emuq* in a bookstore right there in El-Agamy."

Ariel stepped into the middle aisle of the store. She glared at Bernard and pointed to her naked wrist, as though there were a watch on it.

"Ah," said Bernard, "I hate to do this…"

Lucky grinned again. "If I were you," he said, "I would direct those young hormones of yours toward a woman who does not sign your paycheck."

* * *

Ariel's boyfriend Anton arrived shortly after she lowered the metal gate halfway, alerting customers at the mall that the bookstore had closed. Anton moved like a depressed lizard and dressed like a beatnik—turtleneck sweater, skinny jeans, and a beret. Bernard didn't judge others by their appearances, but he found it difficult in Anton's case. He did not consider him a "real" man.

As Bernard straightened books in the fiction section, Anton strolled over and said, "So, what's the latest from Area 51?" Oh, how he would have loved to smack the skinny bastard with a heavy, hardback edition of Stephen King's *The Stand*.

"Not sure what you mean, Anton."

"Ariel told me you're into that stuff." He scratched his neck, then wiped his nose. He could not maintain eye contact. "You know, Big Foot...UFOs...Benghazi."

"What the hell does Benghazi have to do with Big Foot?" said Bernard.

"Chill, bro'," said Anton. "Just making chit chat."

He tried to get away from him. Anton weaseled around the corner and followed him to the entertainment shelf. Bernard separated the music and film titles. He said, "I think Ariel's in the break room."

"No worries." Anton pulled a giant picture book of The Beatles' last American tour and flipped through it. "So overrated," he said.

Bernard stopped. "Excuse me?"

"The Beatles," said Anton. "They're overrated."

Why did he have to listen to this nonsense?

"You don't agree?"

"The Beatles," said Bernard, "whether you like them or not, were brilliant."

Anton looked up long enough to smile, then nodded once more. "It's art, bro'. It's all relative."

Bernard stopped working. "Objectively speaking," he said, "The Beatles were great."

Ariel bounced over to Anton and kissed him on the neck. To Bernard, she said, "What are your plans tonight?" She laughed. "No, wait. What's today? Thursday? Is this the night you get stoned and re-watch *JFK*?"

Well, yeah, it was. "Maybe," said Bernard.

"Oh God," said Anton. "Oliver Stone…overrated."

"You know," said Bernard, "just because our generation hasn't produced any art worth a damn, that doesn't mean we get to shit all over the good stuff from previous generations."

"Boys," said Ariel. She put her arm around Anton's waist. "I think it would be great if you two learned to get along."

Bernard sighed and retreated.

Anton said, "Sorry, babe." He gestured toward Bernard with a lazy finger. "No hard feelings."

"It's cool," said Bernard. "Everybody has their own opinion."

Ariel's eyes widened. "I've got a *killer* idea." She clapped her hands with each syllable she spoke. "Let's get some Chinese, go back to our place, and play like best friends."

Anton brought his eyes up from the floor and glared at her.

"I'm really tired," said Bernard.

"Bullshit," said Ariel. "You know you're going to go home, get high, watch some crazy, paranoid movie. Hang with us instead. Learn how to be social."

Anton urged her to another aisle and they had a quick, quiet conversation. He looked more and more agitated and then relented. He waited there while she returned to the entertainment shelf.

"It's decided," she said to Bernard. "You're chilling with us."

"I got to be here at eight in the morning," he said.

"So do I," she said.

He had never been to his boss's place. He'd imagined it, many times. He'd fantasized one day she'd confess she couldn't contain her lust watching his big butt climb the step-ladder to place excess books on the top shelves. He considered her a good manager—not too bossy, not too lenient. She told him she'd earned an MBA at Valpo. Must have learned compassionate management style there. Or maybe she did it naturally. Whatever society had led him to believe about women in charge, it didn't jibe with the atmosphere she'd created at the bookstore. She was very feminine and he expected her apartment to reflect it—clean, organized, with the sweetest perfume in the air.

His notions of how she lived outside of work, however, disappeared when he stepped into her rat's nest on Fourth Street. Dirty clothes and stacks of coverless paperback books littered the hardwood floors. Mildew and patchouli created a stench he suspected one might smell in hell. He tried not to breathe through his nose. In the kitchen, a pile of dishes in the sink had grown high enough to blend with the counter. Most of the plates had shriveled, brown, nasty cotton balls on them.

They led him to the living room and offered him a seat on a couch covered with food and soda stains. They set the boxes of stir-fried chicken and vegetables on a kidney-shaped coffee table between the couch, an old tube television, and a loveseat whose leather exterior had dulled and cracked. Fresh cotton balls dotted the floor. Ariel's diploma from Valpo hung crooked over the TV. Behind him, three canvases on easels cluttered a hallway leading to, he assumed, their bedroom. They appeared to be unfinished paintings. Ghoulish creatures fondled smaller, more human figures against bleak, dark backgrounds.

"You like those?" Anton sat on the loveseat. He grabbed one of the boxes of stir-fry, opened it, and dug in with his fingers. "I'm coming to grips with some heinous grief I took as a kid," he said.

"Your work?" What a dumb question.

"Yeah, bro'."

He felt terrible for having ever judged the guy. Here was someone *doing* something, as opposed to sitting around and waiting for life to start. Bernard had earned a BA in English at Valpo and discovered no one needed an employee capable of deconstructing David Foster Wallace or Jennifer Egan. He'd habituated himself into an existential lethargy in which he went to work five days a week and spent the rest of his time smoking weed and worrying about Doomsday.

"I think they're great," he said.

"Thanks, bro'." Anton spoke with his mouth full of food.

Ariel emerged from the kitchen with a foggy glass filled with foggier water. "Sorry about the tap." She set the glass on the table in front of Bernard. She joined Anton on the loveseat, smacking his legs so he'd give her space. "Pig," she said to him. Then she dipped her fingers into the stir-fry and fed herself.

Bernard leaned forward and took the other box of food. He unsheathed a set of chopsticks.

Ariel said, "How about a soundtrack?" She found a CD boombox on the floor amidst dirty pants, shirts, and underwear, and tuned the radio to a classic rock station. Aerosmith eviscerated The Beatles' "Come Together."

"Dinosaurs," said Anton.

"Give me a break," she said. "Modern music sucks."

"Scour the Internet," said Anton. "Good stuff is out there. Suits and ties just don't want you listening to anything creative."

"Maybe," said Bernard.

"Whatever," said Ariel.

They finished the food as Bernard and Anton discussed the many ways corporations had ruined the world. Ariel brought out some marijuana for dessert. "Friend of mine got this in Michigan," she said. "Medicinal. Good stuff."

The weed was strong, but not paranoia-inducing. It had a fruity taste and the smoke smelled more like spice than skunk.

And then Anton said to Ariel, "You care if he knows?"

She sighed. "You can't wait?"

He hurried down the hall behind the paintings and returned with a small, wooden box. Celtic patterns had been carved into the edges of it. He sat next to Bernard on the couch. "Hope you don't mind, bro'." He opened the box and took out a syringe with an orange cap on it. He found a spoon on the floor near the coffee table. He dipped the needle into the murky water in the glass Bernard had been drinking from. Then he produced a piece of tin foil from his pocket. He dumped brown powder on the spoon and drained the water from the syringe onto it. Using a lighter, he cooked the drug, employed a fresh cotton ball to sop it up, and pulled the mix into the needle. "Ulcers, bro'," he said. "Had them since I was a kid, you know, because people, you know, they

51

messed with me." He rolled up his sleeve. Brownish-yellow clouds decorated his arms. He tied a belt around his bicep and tapped his skin until he found a workable vein. And then he filled the syringe with his blood, allowing it to bond with the drug, and plunged it back into his body.

"Bernard?" said Ariel.

He looked at her.

"Please don't tell anybody."

"You know I smoke dope like a chimney."

"It's not the same thing," she said.

Anton removed the belt and the needle from his arm. He cradled them in the same hand. His body arched over and sank toward the floor in quick, jerky movements. When he got a hold of himself, he said, "Jesus, even this stuff isn't killing the pain these days."

Lucky insisted Bernard wouldn't be able to handle the demonic trials during the reading of the book, and he certainly couldn't keep a promise to use the gift for altruistic purposes. "Look at you," he said, slapping Bernard's belly. "You're a blimp. You're ruled by your passions."

Once a week, Bernard ate dinner at Ariel's apartment. Anton's paintings developed into vivid representations of abuse. Would they ever hang at the Art Institute in Chicago? Probably not. At least, not for another hundred years. What did people think of Bosch when he first showed his work? The levels of heroin Anton slammed into his blood increased. And yet, Anton said it barely put a layer of relief between him and his ulcers.

"The bathroom these days," he said, "bro', that toilet looks like a *Saw* movie."

Lucky stopped visiting the bookstore. Bernard hoped, at one point, he'd died. He understood why the old man had never read *Emuq*. He was clearly too selfish.

He decided he'd waited long enough the day he'd gone to take a leak in the employee restroom. Ariel had been stripping books to return to the publishers. He'd found her curled atop a sea of romance novel covers, bawling like someone who'd just found out they had a terminal disease. He stood by the wall with the punch clock and posters urging anonymous tips to corporate headquarters. He said, "You okay?"

She used a book cover featuring a shirtless cowboy and fainting woman in a bursting bodice to wipe snot from her nose. "What do you think?"

Kneeling close to her, he said, "Anything you want to talk about?"

She shook her head. "I'm okay."

"Oh." He started to stand. Then he thought better, remembered women didn't always say exactly what they meant. "Are you sure?"

"The idiot's going to kill himself." She used another book cover to straighten her face, smearing eyeliner across her cheeks.

Bernard put his hands in his pockets. Should he get closer and comfort her? Would that be appropriate? She was his boss, after all. She glanced at him. He hated not having a complete understanding of what women wanted. He could *feel* her calling to him. This was a *human* moment, what the hell did rules about work and society matter? She grabbed him and buried her nose in his only nice button-down shirt. She soaked it with tears. Anyone else, he would have been upset.

She spoke into his chest, "Why does he use it if it doesn't work?"

"It's a drug," he said. "It's addictive."

"It was a rhetorical question." She dried her eyes on his sleeve. She leaned back, rested on her palms, and pulled up her nose. "It's killing me, too," she said. "I want to get out of here. Lublin is *nowhere*. I have an MBA, for shit's sake. I should be in Chicago, talking shit in a coffee house or something. I'll be thirty in two years. My life is *over*."

Bernard crossed his legs. He shuffled the scattered book covers closer together. "Why don't you just go?"

"Leave Anton? I've been with him for, like, three years now. That's major, isn't it?"

"I guess." He wondered if Lucky's book applied to both physical and emotional pain. He never wanted to see Ariel like that again. "Why don't you take Anton to Chicago? Seems a better place for an artist."

"Oh, no." She waved her hand as if he'd offered her food she didn't enjoy. "Anton hates Chicago. Calls it a cesspool of violence and phonies."

"It is," said Bernard. "But those phonies love the arts."

"Not going to happen." She pushed herself to her feet. "Who's minding the register?"

Bernard hustled over to Houck's Deli on Vermont during his lunch break. His puke-green Honda sputtered every time he hit the gas pedal. Lucky Camona held court at a table near the dessert display. Three women dressed for office jobs stood around him while he read their fortunes using a deck of cards with esoteric figures and shapes on them.

When Lucky saw him, he frowned. "Can't you take a hint?"

Bernard dragged a metal chair across the floor, leaving marks and causing the young women to cover their ears with their hands. Lucky scowled, as though he actually had a shot with any of them. "I know I can help people," said Bernard. "I don't need to help myself. I don't have any pain."

Lucky tapped the metal table and said, "You're too young, too immature. If you screw it up, get nabbed by unseen hands, who will I complain to about the lack of decent books at your store? Your boss hates me." He looked at the women with a desperate, pathetic smile.

"My lunch hour is up in fifteen minutes," said Bernard. "I don't return on time, I might get fired anyway."

The old man said, "No. Absolutely not."

Bernard crossed his arms and sat back, prompting a groan from his chair. "I'm not leaving until you agree to let me read the book."

He picked up Lucky the following Saturday morning. The old man had instructed him to avoid partying the night before, to get a good rest, and to eat a solid breakfast. "You're going to need all the energy you can muster," he said. He'd wrapped the book in a brown paper bag and held it close to his chest. He told him to drive to Pawpaw Grove.

They took I-65 to State Road 231 and crossed Canopy Road, lined for miles by fiery Red Maples grown so close together they formed a natural tunnel. Lucky directed him to park in a lot between Dairy Queen, the only business in town, and a two-story brownstone. It looked like it had been built in the early 1800s. The letters F and U had been painted in white between the first and second floors. "Fallers Union," said Lucky. "Never you mind what you've heard about us. The Fallers haven't had any influence since the end of the Second World War. Now it's just me and a lot of other coots sitting around yapping about how great things used to be." He got out and carried the book under his arm.

As Lucky produced a crowded key ring from a pocket in his beige windbreaker, a cool, October breeze disturbed loose bricks in the walls of the lodge. He tried several keys in the small, wooden front door, before finding one that worked. The lock clicked and he said, "Give me a hand." The hinges creaked like they hadn't been oiled in a decade. Bernard used his shoulder to force it open. Lucky walked past him and turned on the lights.

Thin, painted, crooked circles, like rings in a tree, diminished to the center of the marble floor in the reception hall. He followed Lucky to a set of pale doors with gold trim. "This is the temple." He opened the doors and said, "Look into the darkness."

Bernard stepped into the pitch-black room. He could smell carpet cleaner and polished leather. Lucky flipped a light switch behind him. Three rows of fine, fold-down theater seats occupied the long sides of the room. At the far end, a giant, wood-carved chair dominated a low stage. Murals of lumberjacks cutting trees covered the walls. Bernard had read about the Fallers Union. They were rumored to worship a god called Jarilo, to have engineered both world wars, and to have caused the social, cultural, and economic collapse of Western Civilization. Any time a secret society received credit for too many evils, he assumed they were, more than likely, benevolent.

Lucky led him to an altar in the center featuring a Bible and three unused candles. He set down the book and left the room. Bernard thought about peeking, but stopped himself. He'd made it this far. No need to piss off Lucky.

The old man returned with a wooden chair appropriate for a dining table in a Norman Rockwell painting. He placed it before the altar and told Bernard to sit. "Understand," he said, "when I leave and I lock that door," he pointed to the entrance to the temple, "and you open this book and begin reading it out loud, you may not stop, you may not take a break. No matter how terrible things get, you must read it to the very end without *any* interruption *what-so-ever.*"

"It's cool," said Bernard.

Lucky shook his head. "I don't know..."

"I'll do what you say."

Lucky produced a matchbook and lit the candle closest to Bernard. "Finish before it burns out." And then he cut the lights and closed and locked the doors behind him.

Bernard unwrapped the book, tossing the paper bag to the side. It had been composed of a sticky, rubbery material, like stretched and dried human skin. The Babylonian word for power, *Emuq*, had been written in blood on the cover and the spine. As he opened it to the first, thick page, it sounded like a pile of brittle bones crushing under pressure. The book only had nine pages. "Piece of cake," he said. The dry, flaking print was in Latin. He read, pronouncing the words as best as he could recall from his high school etymology class—

Stellae autem ratione alligned

The floor beneath his chair rumbled. He assured himself it had only been his imagination. In the darkness, he thought he saw the form of a naked woman, dancing in rhythm to the bouncing candlelight. She had short, bobbed hair. He almost said, "Ariel?" but stopped himself. He turned to the next page—

Sunt opus insanientis

Furious tapping inside the walls reminded him of growing up in a house infested with rodents. He'd see them race across the kitchen floor every day. He remembered the only food his parents could afford—Twinkies and soda and pizzas. The kitchen had always been stocked with Little Debbie's and Hostess Cup Cakes and his parents, who were never around, told him to take care of himself. He'd been slim until puberty, when the junk food caught up with him. By high school, he'd gotten grotesquely overweight. Girls would have nothing to do with him. Marijuana became his mistress. *And you think you can heal others?* It wasn't his voice. He ignored his doubts and continued—

Finditur in procella spatium

Somewhere between him and the door to the temple, invisible hinges groaned like the last notes of an orchestra whose members had died at the very same instant. He imagined acquiring the power to heal and finding a way to profit from it. *Yes, yes!* He saw a mansion, *yes*, a *mansion*. What kind of car would he drive, now that he had a path to riches? What would all the people who'd ever doubted him say when they saw him on television, healing like a preacher? He could print his own copies of the book and sell them. *Yes, yes, yes! Do it!* More alien thoughts, planted in his head. He ignored them and moved on—

Hic iacet in occultis, ut sanctitas

From nowhere, a light wind tossed his hair from his eyes. It quickly built and he sensed the temple had filled with demons. The wind itself did not howl, rather, it rode the chatter of creatures speaking in ancient tongues. They talked of his parents, how they'd settled for terrible service jobs that barely paid the rent. How they gorged themselves on the same crappy food they forced him to eat. How they'd gotten cancer and died before he'd finished high school. When he refused to attend his father's funeral, the priest from St. Bridget's admonished him. Who the hell was he to say a goddamn word to him? He hadn't grown up in that shithole, alone, his parents insisting there was no God, no heaven, no purpose in life other than working and dying. Where was that priest now? How he'd like to find him and beat the ever-loving bejesus out of him. No, no. Bernard Horvat was paranoid and undisciplined. Not angry. He wanted to tell the demons, "Nice try." But even that would constitute a victory for them. He returned his focus to the book—

Missa in tempore, et in mythologia

Whatever or whomever had joined him in the temple now ran circles around him. The cacophony of dead languages created a whirlwind. They informed him his parents had been correct, there was no heaven. But, they said, there is most certainly a hell, and that's where they are now. They showed him—a light tore through the darkness and opened a view of a concrete tomb where barely visible humanoid creatures shrieked as flames engulfed them. In the center, he recognized his mother and father, separated by only a few feet, screaming for mercy. The demons informed him this had been his parents' punishment for the words they'd spoken against the Great Creator. *You can save them, yes you can. Stand and go to them, you may free them of this eternal torture.* He grabbed the book tighter and forced himself to continue—

Qui sapit diem mortis aeternum erit

Fingers, some thin and bony, some meaty and slimy, grasped at him. They got through, every now and then, slapping his face, trying to tilt his eyes away from the pages of the book. They hissed in his ears, claiming they'd find anyone he'd ever loved and shred them. They told him the name of his boss, Ariel. They said they would rip her apart in an act so violent the writers of history would dwell on her fate for the rest of time. Then, they threatened *him*. They begged him to consider what it would feel like to have his arms turned backwards and slowly removed from their sockets, inch-by-inch, hour-by-hour. How much fun they would have, slicing into his fat belly and pulling out his intestines while he watched. Could he appreciate what destruction they were capable of? No. He had no interest. He read on—

Universi requirit pupillam!

The beasts clawing at his skin, trying to rip his eyes from their sockets, offered to give him the power to heal without having to read the entire book. After all, they said, you are not *really* interested in helping anyone other than yourself. You are what you have accused many others of being: a phony. *You pretend to care about the pain of the artist Anton, but your sights are and always have been on the woman, Ariel. You say Yes Ma'am and No Ma'am when she gives you instructions at work, as though you respect her authority, but you cannot wait to go home and fantasize all the ways you would penetrate her, given the opportunity.* No, he was no fraud. Not at all. He would help Anton so that someone from his generation could finally produce art worth talking about. He flipped to the next page—

TIBI UNUM, ET IDEM!

A thousand hands grabbed his flesh and pulled. They kicked at his feet to knock him over. They rocked the altar and forced him to stop them from stealing the candle. The temple glowed blue and white as a lake of ice developed beneath his chair. His parents glared at him, frozen, their eyes locked in accusatory sorrow. Had his belief in God condemned them? No. No. No. He turned to the last page. Demons clutched his jaw, forced their fingers inside his mouth and tried to remove his tongue—

TU ES DEUS!!!

The candlelight flashed and disappeared. He closed the book. The commotion in the room halted. He stuffed the book back into the brown paper bag. As he felt his way through the dark, trying to find the door, a low wheezing, like a balloon losing air, travelled by him and disappeared somewhere near the chair on the stage.

The old man looked at him as though he were an alien. His ancient skull tilted left and right, his eyes roamed up and down Bernard, perhaps expecting tentacles to burst from his chest or his skin to melt away and reveal some deformed, hideous creature. "I'm guessing things went okay," he said.

"You didn't hear the racket?" said Bernard.

"Nope." He urged him to step out of the temple so he could close the doors. He motioned for him to give him the book. "Whatever you experienced, it happened only in your mind." He led him to the entrance of the lodge. His wingtips smacked the marble floor in the lobby and echoed throughout the building. Before they exited, he stopped and said, "You mess it up, boy, those monsters will become real."

They didn't say anything else as they got into Bernard's crappy Honda and he drove them toward I-65. Lucky rested his head against the window and napped. He snored like a four-hundred-pound beast. Bernard turned on the radio, found the college station from Valpo. Some band he'd never heard of played the same two chords for five minutes, repeated the same phrase. Steel guitar collided with a hip-hop beat and a twangy singer running scales like Mariah Carey. Was it country? Was it pop? He questioned

Anton's claim that their generation could make great music. Then he slammed his foot onto the break pedal.

Lucky flew forward, nearly hit his head on the dashboard. His seatbelt snapped him back. His sunglasses landed crooked on his face.

In the middle of the road, a battered doe beat the pavement with her front hooves. Her head flailed as she screeched in pain. Bernard put the car in park. He took off his seat belt and opened his door.

"Just drive around it," said Lucky. "Someone will come along and finish it off."

Bernard checked for traffic as he got out. He approached the animal slowly, not wanting to agitate it. The doe's cries resembled a cartoon donkey. Her hooves clacked like a woman in high heels rushing down a sidewalk. The animal leaned away from him. He knelt next to her, out of the range of her hooves. "You're going to be okay," he said. She switched her shrieks to a low grunt, as though warning him. He put his hand on her neck. She twitched, resisted. Something passed through him, like a wave in his blood. Not so physical, rather, emotional.

The doe breathed slower and rested her head on the highway. The passenger door opened, and Lucky stood behind him.

"Want to give me a hand?" Bernard nodded at the animal.

"Let nature fix it," said Lucky.

Bernard removed his jacket, considered it a small sacrifice. He wrapped it around the doe's disfigured hind legs and scooped her into his arms. He placed her in the tall grass on the side of the road.

Lucky produced a black, scratched pistol from inside his windbreaker. He aimed at the doe's head and pulled the trigger. Two pops disrupted the air like children's fireworks. The animal stopped moving. Her eyes reflected the clouds as a puddle of blood formed underneath her.

Bernard understood what Lucky had done. It didn't make watching it any easier.

"Taking away her pain wouldn't have saved her life," said the old man.

* * *

After dropping off Lucky at Houck's Deli, Bernard drove to Ariel's apartment. He expected Anton to be there. When he knocked on the door, his boss opened it. She had a tissue in her hand. "Hey," she said.

"Thought you'd be at the store."

"I had to take Anton to St. Mary's." She walked back into the apartment without inviting him to join her.

Bernard said, "What's going on?" He stepped over the books and clothes in the front hallway and followed her to the living room.

She plopped down on the couch amidst a sea of used Kleenex. She pulled more from a box on the coffee table. "Jesus," she said, "I wish I weren't such a sap."

As he swept used tissues to the floor, Bernard sat next to her. "You going to tell me what's going on?"

She shook her head. "Oh God," she said. "He went into the bathroom this morning and screamed. Blood all over the place, like a massacre. I called 911. They told me it'd be faster if I drove him to Haggard myself." She fell into him, draped her arms around his belly.

He hesitated, wondering what putting his hands on her would do at that point. She hadn't worn pants, just a long Snoopy t-shirt. He could feel her legs against his. He held her and rubbed her arm. The wave passed through him again. He shivered. His mother would have told him someone had walked over his grave.

Ariel's breathing slowed. She asked him, "I ever tell you about my last boyfriend?"

He said she had not.

"Did his thing in Afghanistan for three years," she said. "Told me he was coming home for good. Then I see on the news he was shot at a café the day before he was supposed to get on a plane for Germany." She sat up and glared at him. "Strange," she said. "I don't feel anything right now."

Bernard looked over his shoulder, as though she might be addressing someone else.

"I must be the Angel of Death," she said.

He tried to pretend he hadn't noticed her nipples, announcing themselves on either side of Snoopy's grinning face. He tried not to stare at her thighs, tried not to think about whether or not she'd worn panties. "So, why aren't you at the hospital?"

She shook her head. "I can't sit in that room with him, watching bullshit television. If he's awake, he just whines. It's too much." She picked at the bottom of her shirt. "Normally, I feel guilty, you know, worrying about myself instead of him." She looked at his hands. "For some reason, you don't make me feel that way." She stared at him until he thought she'd lean in and kiss him.

He stood and said, "Why don't we go see him?"

"Who?"

He pointed to Anton's paintings on the easels.

"What for?" She made a sour face, like she'd bitten into a clove of garlic.

"Look," he said, "I'm going to drive over to St. Mary's, see if the guy needs anything. Maybe he doesn't want to eat that healthy crap they serve, maybe he'd like something to read."

"What are you talking about?" She put her hands on her hips, hoisting her t-shirt high enough to reveal torn, pink panties.

Bernard forced himself to maintain eye contact with her. "Maybe I can pick up some dinner for you on the way back?"

He parked in the visitor's lot at St. Mary's. The giant cross posted on the front of the building glowed against an overcast sky. At a desk just beyond the sliding doors, a receptionist wearing a knit shawl and horn-rimmed glasses helped him locate Anton's floor and room number. She looked like the organist at his grandfather's church.

"Can he have visitors?" he asked.

She told him to go to the fourth floor and check in there.

On the elevator, a middle-aged woman and her grown daughter discussed how ready they were for the older woman's mother to die. "I haven't had a weekend to myself in six months," she said. Bernard wondered if her anger represented a kind of pain. If he touched her arm, would she value her mother? Did she not know how terrible she'd feel once her mother was gone?

The receptionist on the fourth floor pointed him to Anton's

room. She said he'd just woken up. "Nurses are through with him. He should be good now."

The corridor smelled like disinfectant and cough syrup. Nurses and orderlies, their hands wrapped in rubber gloves, lugged soiled sheets, specimen bottles, full bedpans, and other things Bernard would never take money to touch. *Selfish*, he reminded himself. Not a good thing.

The television in Anton's room blared. The phony voice of a newscaster promised to reveal something deadly "that might be in your household at this very moment." Several nurses glanced at his door and sneered.

Bernard entered the room. Curtains on a half-circle track surrounded a toilet near Anton's bed. The TV had been mounted on an arm that stretched and pivoted. Anton lay on his side in a hospital gown, clutching his stomach.

"Christ." He squeezed the words through clenched teeth. He turned his head, maybe realizing he wasn't alone.

"TV's loud," said Bernard.

Anton waved his hand in front of his nose, as though he'd gotten a whiff of something horrible. "Don't want anybody to hear me cry," he said.

"They told me the nurses had taken care of you." Bernard pointed at several bags of fluid hanging on an IV pole. "They haven't given you anything for the pain?"

"That shit doesn't work." He said he'd told them about his heroin use, not that he'd ever be able to hide it. Their answer, according to him, was to give him maximum doses of morphine every three hours. "Imagine someone shooting King Kong with a BB gun and expecting him to die. It ain't happening, bro'." He winced and pushed at his belly, as though he were trying to separate his insides.

Bernard asked if the doctors had told him what the problem might be. Anton said they weren't sure yet. "They think it's burst. Who the hell knows? Normally, I can keep the pain around five or six. This morning, the amp went straight to eleven."

"You mind if I turn this down?" Bernard nodded at the television.

"Really, bro', I don't want them constantly coming in here and asking me, in all seriousness, if I'm okay."

The remote control rested on a sink between the bed and a window with the shades drawn. Bernard snatched it before Anton could. He aimed it at the TV and hit the 'mute' button. "I hate seeing you like this," he said.

"What's it got to do with you?"

"Ariel," he said. "She's the best boss I've had so far and it's tearing her up, watching you live like this." He thought of being on the couch with her, seeing her thighs, smelling her unwashed skin.

"Oh, jeez," said Anton. "I mean, I dig her okay, but she spends all her time sulking about how her life went sour because patriarchal bastards wouldn't give her a shot in business."

Bernard peeked through the crack between the shades and the window. The sun had fled behind a colony of clouds against an electric blue sky. He'd risked his life reading the book to help Anton and he wondered whether or not the guy would appreciate it. "You need anything?" he said.

"Life without my intestines would be awesome right about now."

"What are they feeding you?"

"Apple sauce."

"How about some pizza, a burger maybe?"

"Are you kidding?" Anton gawked at him. "Do you know what an ulcer is?"

"The TV going to get you through?" said Bernard. "You know, entertainment-wise?"

Anton took a deep breath. "Bro'," he said, "I know your heart's in the right place. My existence, at this moment, is excruciating pain. I can't feel anything else. I don't care about anything else. I wish I were dead."

Bernard put his hand on Anton's shoulder. "All right." He kept it there, despite the confused look on Anton's face. An ice-cold shiver snaked through his body, down his arm, and out of his palm. He stepped back.

"What the hell did you just do?" Anton flapped his hands near his belly, as though he wanted to fly away. "It's gone," he said. "Everything is gone." He sat up and stared at him the way Bernard's mother did the day he told her he believed in God.

"You can get some rest," said Bernard. "Maybe watch TV at a reasonable volume." He tried to give him the remote control.

Anton slapped it out of his hand. It flew across the room and skidded over the shiny, polished floor. The back broke and two triple-A batteries rolled in different directions. "Are you stupid?" he said. "No pain, no art."

Bernard grabbed a pair of Italian subs from Houck's Deli on the way to Ariel's apartment. He didn't know what to expect from her when he got back to her place. She'd looked like a zombie before he'd left earlier, standing in the middle of her living room, just glaring at him. He grabbed his order from the cashier and tried to walk past Lucky Camona without getting his attention.

Lucky stretched his leg in the aisle to stop him. Despite it being night, the old man wore his sunglasses. He shook his finger at the food in Bernard's hands. "Two sandwiches?" he said. He patted Bernard's belly. "Mind your passions, boy."

Bernard said thanks and pushed past him. He felt as though he'd done something wrong, though he knew damn well he hadn't. The refurbished engine in his crappy Honda protested as he sped away from Houck's. The only person he trusted, at that point, was Ariel. He parked crooked outside her building and rushed up the stairs.

When she saw the food, she said, "Neat." She moseyed through the hallway to the kitchen. "You need a plate, or you want to eat it straight from the bag, like a bum?"

He said, "Anton's better. He'll sleep well, I think."

She cleared dirty cotton balls off a pair of plates. She ran water over the dishes for half a second and used a fungus-stained washcloth to dry them. She handed one to him and said, "Wonder how long it will last."

They ate on the couch in the living room. When they finished their food, they sat next to each other, saying nothing. He might as well have been at home, alone. What was he waiting for? The wind picked up outside her window. It sounded like a motor, revving, until he turned his head and studied Anton's paintings.

Ariel fell asleep and he soon followed. When her phone rang at three in the morning, he had to push her head off his lap. She tumbled to the floor, knocking her hip on the coffee table. "Shit," she said. She crawled through the landscape of clothes and cotton balls. She'd set the ringtone to a high-pitched chirping, like a parakeet. The longer she went without finding it, the more it sliced into Bernard's nerves. She found it under the loveseat and answered it. She listened and then said, "Oh, I see." She hung up. "We got to go," she said to Bernard.

He waited for her to explain.

She said, "They told me a chaplain would meet us at the entrance."

He'd seen them, just outside the car, on the way to and from the hospital. Nothing monstrous, just sharp, shifting shadows belonging to no one, crawling along the edges of buildings and sidewalks. Ariel drove them in a VW bug her parents had bought her when she'd been graduated from high school in 2007. A dead rose arched out of the flower-holder on the dashboard. The radio station from Valpo played retro alternative music—Joy Division, Echo & the Bunnymen, This Mortal Coil, songs suggesting depression had been invented in England during the 1970s and 80s.

When they arrived, a minister who looked older than Lucky Camona greeted them near the elevators. He carried a Bible under his arm and rode with them to the fourth floor. Ariel asked Bernard to wait in the reception area. She and the priest disappeared into Anton's room and didn't come out for nearly an hour. Bernard thought he might be able to hear a heart-rate monitor, something beeping, like in the movies. The only noise, however, came from televisions in other patients' rooms.

On the way to Ariel's apartment afterwards, she said Anton's stomach had bled out. "Doctor assured me he was in peace, promised he felt no pain." She shook her head. "I find that difficult to believe."

Bernard asked if she wanted to be alone.

"You understand my boyfriend just died?"

He sat on her couch by himself while she washed her face and changed into a Hello Kitty t-shirt and a pair of black short-shorts. When she joined him in the living room, she lowered her head onto his lap. He touched her arm and felt a slower, calmer wave travel from his body to hers.

"We're just friends, right?"

He said, "What do *you* want?"

She put her hand on his cheek and pulled him closer.

Ariel begged him not to judge her, which, he assured her, would be impossible. They made love three times before the sun carved red lines around patched drapes on her windows. They fell asleep on the floor, amidst the clothes and cotton balls. She woke before he did. He watched her dial her cell phone and convey the news to Anton's parents, who lived in Chicago, that their son had passed away. When she hung up, she said, "They sound even less surprised than me."

He wanted to tell her she *should* be surprised, that he'd meddled with her, prevented her from feeling sorrow. And he'd begun to suspect something worse—that he'd known, unconsciously, removing Anton's pain would thwart his ability to recognize when his ulcer had become deadly.

Eventually, Ariel took a shower and announced, "I've got to meet his parents at the hospital."

"Should I call you later?"

"I don't know." The way she crossed her arms when she said it, he assumed she meant no.

In his crappy Honda, on the way back to his apartment, shadows reeled in the corners of his eyes. He turned up the radio, shouted along to a Guns 'n' Roses song. It did nothing to drown a steady drone he'd heard since the early morning, since he'd first kissed Ariel and helped her undress. The sound reminded him of going to midnight mass with his grandpa. The organist with horn-rimmed glasses would rest her fingers on low notes while the congregation filed in. He stopped singing and shouted, "*She* wanted it, dammit."

As he parked outside his building, frantic shadows roiled on the dull, orange exterior. The droning noise got louder. He ran to the front door. Invisible hands ripped his sweat-soaked shirt. He forced his way inside and slammed the glass doors.

He pressed the button for the elevator, saw it would be coming from the top floor, and raced to the stairs instead. As he hustled to the first landing, the heavy door to the stairwell banged shut. Shadows swirled up the steps from below. Others descended from the next level. They swarmed the walls around him. The droning became a deafening wail. Darkness swallowed him. Pressure squeezed him from all angles and with a sloppy pop and squish, his blood streamed from his body as his bones splintered like brittle twigs.

Ariel Grimes took her time shelving new copies of The Koran. She constantly peered around the corner of the religion shelf to make sure no customers had entered the store. Her new employee, a bundle of high school energy named Brittany, wasn't scheduled to come in until noon. She'd have the girl arrange the mystery section and keep an eye on the counter while she hid from the world in the break room.

Losing her boyfriend Anton had made sense. At least, that's how she found peace in the fact that she had yet to shed a tear since he'd died. Not many attended the funeral. His parents, siblings, and cousins looked appropriately upset. She'd sat through the service and the burial wondering where the hell Bernard had gone. He seemed so concerned about Anton's health. And he'd slept with her, made love to her like it had been the only thing he'd ever wanted from life. And then he vanished. No phone call, no two-week notice.

She knew having sex the night she'd learned her boyfriend had passed would never look good on her ethics resume, but she didn't feel guilty. And normally, if a guy went to bed with her and never called again, she'd be furious. But she didn't care. She straightened out the goofy books Bernard used to pluck from the weirdo shelf in the religion section and talk about endlessly after reading them. Thanks to him, she'd become familiar with all manner of lore she had no interest in—Ruby Ridge, the Loch Ness Monster, etc.

She recognized the titles, the authors, and then stopped at a pale-shaded book she'd never seen. The spine had no publisher's logo, no ISBN code, just four random letters. She pulled it out and ran her fingers over it. The book had been constructed from a pliable, rubbery material. On the cover, the same word from the spine, *Emuq*, had been written in dark, red ink. It looked like chipped and flaking blood. She had no recollection of cataloging and shelving it. Must have been something Bernard ordered and entered into the computer without her knowing. A parting reminder of his stupid, paranoid interests.

STUCK

Jessica convinced Emily to trip on Ghost. She'd researched it before trying it herself. She'd dropped a hit under the guidance of her boyfriend, Kale. She called it a "life flipper." Whatever that meant. She said she no longer feared death. This appealed to Emily. She'd spent the second semester of her junior year sitting in her room, staring at a framed picture of her and her boyfriend Travis taken at homecoming—him in his jersey, the thin, goofy mustache he'd been trying to grow sticking out like a caterpillar, and her in a navy blue dress bought for the dance they never attended. After he died, his parents gave her his smartphone and she listened to the pop songs on it over and over, washing her pillow with tears every Friday and Saturday night. Jessica said when she took Ghost, she'd seen her father who'd been shot to death outside the downtown Dairy Queen two years ago. She said she'd waved to him, but resisted the urge to hug him. "Kale told me not to make contact with the ghosts," she said. "He told me a friend of his cousin in Mausten did that and got stuck."

She'd known Jessica since kindergarten. Anything she could get in trouble for, Jessica had introduced her to it. Alcohol? Fifth grade. Jessica's dad was still alive. She'd stolen five cans of Schlitz from him and crammed them into her *Batman* backpack for a sleepover. They finished three before Emily ralphed out her window into her mother's patch of gardenias. They both felt sick the next day. Never touched the stuff afterward. Not even at parties Travis took

71

her to where the Rah-Rahs guzzled beer from kegs. He gave her static for it, called her a spaz in front of their friends. In private, he told her he respected her for not being a clone. "You're my little rebel," he'd said. Maybe not the most accurate assessment, considering she followed the same *Cosmo* trends every other Rah-Rah did.

Later, Jessica discovered weed. Seventh grade. Her father convinced her to try it. She invited Emily over soon after. "It makes music sound like marshmallows," she'd said. Emily had no idea what that meant. They smoked from a glass bong shaped like a wizard, the wizard's hands cupping the bowl. She'd raided her father's CD collection and played a band called the Beastie Boys. "Listen to the bass," she'd said. "It'll pick you up and float you around the room." But the drug never kicked in for Emily. She'd sat there bored while Jessica rolled on the floor in hysterics. The more she complained about it, the harder Jessica laughed.

Sophomore year, the Halloween after her father had been killed for, allegedly, sleeping with Don Horan's wife, she'd gotten her to try mushrooms. "You're going to take a walk in your mind," she'd said. They prepared tea. It smelled like poop and tasted like dirt. Forty-five minutes later, her thoughts raced and music jumped to life. They listened to more old people stuff, some group called XTC. Sounded like The Beatles. She considered them overrated. She'd just started dating Travis then and already knew he was The One. He'd told her The Beatles weren't relevant. He read *Rolling Stone*, which meant he knew about things like that. The layered voices from the XTC record sent streams of colors twisting and turning before her eyes. Something about 'drowning' in 'summer's cauldron,' whatever that meant. Too weird. She'd asked if they could listen to something good, something *new*. The groups from the last century didn't understand the complexity of simplicity. Travis had told her that as well. She considered it the smartest thing she'd ever heard. She repeated it to Jessica, who then embarked on an epic laughing jag. A half hour into the trip, Emily feared she'd gone insane. Jessica got serious for a moment and assured her, "You haven't done enough to get stuck."

She'd survived mushrooms, aside from watching awful, ancient music draw cartoons on the walls. A small price to pay for hanging out with Jessica, who didn't dress or act like her other friends. She wore dark clothes and painted her nails black. Looked like she should be dating Edgar Allan Poe. And she'd been the most supportive after Travis died.

He'd played receiver for the Haggard Steelers and took what *The Times* called a "high-low shot." Died on the field. The paper said he suffered blunt trauma to the spine. She'd seen him take similar tackles for two years. He'd always popped back up and said something nasty to the other team, acting like it didn't hurt. Homecoming, however, he'd flopped to the ground like a sack of potatoes. Just laid there, not moving. The worst she figured would be paralysis. Her father had warned her something like that could happen. The medics cut the facemask off his helmet and strapped him to a gurney. Minutes after the ambulance for St. Joseph's pulled onto the field and carried him away, Mrs. Gretchen, her history teacher, tapped her on the shoulder and suggested she meet Travis's family at the hospital. As she drove her father's pickup to St. Joseph's, she visualized holding Travis's hand. A voice from deep inside, however, told her what she didn't want to believe—that she'd never hear him speak again, say profound things about music and shopping, never feel him put his arms around her and rub her back right in the middle, her sweet spot that relaxed her and made her forget the stress of school and living with her clueless parents. She'd turned up the radio to drown her thoughts and sang along with the latest booty anthem.

A month after the funeral, when the condolences and cards from her Rah-Rah friends stopped, when the first whispers of, "Jeez, why doesn't she get on with her life?" floated down the halls of Haggard High, only Jessica continued asking her, every day, "How are you doing?" She belonged to the Bacos, the town stoners, the exact opposite of the Rah-Rahs. Emily's parents had groomed her since kindergarten to attend Notre Dame or Brown or, at worst, Michigan. Jessica's future involved technical college, though even that seemed unlikely as she sank into the drug culture and ditched school every day. Emily took loads of grief from the Rah-Rahs for hanging out with her. They'd even tried an intervention. Her stupid mother had encouraged them, let them into the living room. Some major *Dr. Phil* crap. Travis, his football buddies, and all the Rah-Rahs hugged her and cried and called Jessica the spawn of Satan.

After Travis died, only Jessica showed up with buckets of Rocky Road ice cream on Friday nights. Emily had wanted nothing but to stay at home and feel sorry for herself, curse Travis for dying, curse the defensive backs from East Chicago for hitting him, and curse God for letting her pain be part of His grand, selfish, cosmic plan. Jessica wouldn't let her. She brought her father's ancient VCR along with stacks of giant, VHS boxes containing the silliest comedies from the 1980s. Always the same story—nerd likes popular girl, nerd gets date with popular girl, nerd realizes popular girl is an air-head, nerd falls in love with local Tomboy instead. Emily had suggested she find something better to do with her time.

"Nonsense," she'd said. "You want me to stay at home and listen to my aunt tell me the same old stories about Pa-pa? What a bum he was for getting killed before I could support myself? I've heard it a thousand times already."

Shortly before spring break, she suggested Emily try Ghost. Said Kale had turned her on to it. Jessica had met Kale in Chicago. He played bass for The Feelings Patrol, a folk-rock band Travis would have despised. He had one of those bizarre haircuts with the sides shaved and the top moussed and folded over. He'd also grown a full beard that needed to be trimmed and tamed. He wore cowboy boots, skinny jeans, knit sweaters and a scarf, even when the weather called for shorts and a t-shirt. He insisted anyone who disagreed with him on *anything* was stupid and would get their ass kicked if they pissed him off. Travis would've flattened him with little effort, but, whatever. Jessica liked him. Probably a reaction to her father, who'd been an old school alpha-male.

Jessica showed Emily what she'd read about Ghost on the Internet. If you made contact with a spirit while you were under the drug's influence, you took its place and it moved on to heaven or hell or wherever. Jessica repeated the instructions when she and Kale showed up with a hit for her. "You get stuck on Ghost," she said, "you're *really* stuck, like, surfing eternity. Know what I'm saying?"

Emily said she'd changed her mind. "Mushrooms were scary enough."

Jessica reminded her she'd be able to see Travis. "Isn't that worth it?"

She resented her using Travis to twist her arm. How could she say no? She'd wanted to see him every day since homecoming, even if just to say goodbye. If she didn't at least try, she'd regret it the rest of her life. "All right, all right," she said. Part of her hoped maybe she *would* get stuck, providing it didn't feel anything like the mushroom craziness. She wouldn't have to worry about making good grades anymore, about looking like the latest model on the cover of *Cosmo*, about pleasing everyone but herself. How great would it be, not to have to stand in front of the mirror in her bathroom in hot outfits and snap new selfies every week? The whole routine seemed useless once she didn't have Travis holding her hand in the hallways of Haggard High.

Jessica told her to lean back on her bed. "We're going to be here the whole time." She explained that Emily would put the small tablet underneath her tongue and let it dissolve. "It'll feel like Pop Rocks, popping like soda bubbles." She said the drug kicked in much faster than mushrooms. She said her heart would speed up right away, not to worry about it. "You'll phase out," she said, "but I want you to relax. That's your conscious mind leaving your body." She said when she stepped outside, she'd see *them*.

"Who?" said Emily.

Kale chimed in with smug tones jerks from Chicago affected when talking to people from Indiana—"Duh, genius." He flipped the goofy sliver of hair in his eyes to the side. "Why do you think they call it Ghost?"

Jessica continued advising her: "Remember what the Internet said—you're going to see dead people at the moment they cashed in. It's kind of like they're stuck. Not old people who died naturally, but young people, like us, you know, normal people who died suddenly, without warning."

Emily looked at the small, folded piece of aluminum in Jessica's hand. "Did you get to say goodbye to your dad?"

"I don't know if he heard me," she said. "It was for me, though. Saying goodbye, you know? I wanted to get closer…" She nodded over her shoulder. "Dummy here warned me not to."

Kale scratched at his beard as though he'd lost something in it. "My cousin totally knows this dude from Wisconsin who tried to hug his dead sister. Bro's heart stopped beating. People who took Ghost after that said they saw him hanging from the same rafter in their attic his sister had used to kill herself."

"You guys believe that?" said Emily.

Jessica shrugged. "If you go to the highway, you can see where Mr. Shipwick's wife's car got smashed by that semi. Or you can take State Road 53 into town and see Donny Gross get run over by that bull, over there at the Franklin farm, you remember that?"

"Why would I want to see that?"

Jessica shrugged. She unfolded the aluminum. "Now," she said, gently pushing Emily toward her pillow, "close your eyes, stick out your tongue."

Emily stopped her. "I don't know."

"Good Christ." Kale paced the room with his hands on his hips, stared at the ceiling. "This is how I'm wasting my Friday night?"

"Ignore him." Jessica forced the tablet under Emily's tongue. "If you get scared, just remind yourself—it'll be over in less than hour."

The words wobbled in her ears as tiny explosions tickled her mouth. Her heart thundered. She tried to spit the tablet out, but it had already dissolved. Jessica put her hand on her shoulder. "Relax," she said, so quiet Emily almost didn't hear. She forced herself to lay still. Her heart pounded louder, stronger. The edges of her bed, her desk, and the office chair she sat in to do her homework glowed purple. The walls throbbed, as though breathing. The forms of Jessica and tall, lanky, stupid Kale flashed over her like dying neon signs. A low drone, the kind her father's stereo amplifier made when switched on, rattled the window, rumbled from the floor. She imagined something fierce rising from the earth, threatening to bust into her room and devour her. She rose to see if she could silence it. Her movements were fluid, as though she were gliding through the air.

When she reached the window, the hunger to see Travis calmed her fear of the droning noise. She melted through the panes, hovered over her mother's patch of gardenias below, and coasted to the ground. The houses, trees, cars parked in the street and driveways, all bathed in a deep, rich purple. They faded and reappeared quickly, offering glimpses of what the land must have looked like before it was turned into suburban Haggard. Lights burned inside the two-story, brick homes. Shadows danced behind the curtains and shades. She moved to her father's pickup, tried to put her hand on it, but felt nothing.

A shriek travelled the air from the Johnson's house, down the street. She'd heard a previous owner, a man named Hop Robbins, shot his wife and three children in the Johnson's house in the 1970s, during the strike at Liberty Steel. He'd been laid off for participating in the walkout and decided he couldn't take it anymore. Emily's curiosity tugged her toward the Tudor-style home. Large, round windows in the front looked like eyes. Everyone considered the place haunted. Everyone except for the Johnsons, who had to live there. The brown cross-beams split the windows and every ten seconds, the shriek sliced the air again and a woman in a brown skirt and lacy, pink blouse, probably Hop Robbins' wife, flew through the left window and landed on the gravel walkway leading to the door. The first time it happened, Emily tried to scream, but made no sound. The woman stood, examined the gash torn in her chest by the shotgun blast, brushed herself off, and stormed back into the house. The sequence became rhythmic, like a good drum beat— Shriek, gunshot, woman out the window, repeat, repeat, repeat.

Emily wanted to help her, somehow. She approached the walkway and waited for the woman to appear again. When the woman stood, she turned and smiled. She opened her arms. Emily started toward her, then stopped. She forced herself into the street and headed for Haggard High, pretending the woman's cries for mercy didn't exist.

She took State Road 53, per Jessica's suggestion. Donny Gross, a comic book geek whose parents were rumored alcoholics, had been trampled by a bull named Mojo in junior high. She'd forgotten about him. Everyone had. The Franklin property had been converted into an alternative energy farm. Giant, white windmills loomed over the trees. They shivered inside rich, purple borders painted by the drug. Grain towers long gone appeared and disappeared. Emily imagined a clock somewhere, turning fast, like in a cartoon, and time going round and round as animals and tractors and men working in the fields popped up and then vanished in less than a second. It made her dizzy, nauseous.

Donny Gross, still twelve years old, rode in from the opposite direction. He picked his nose and stuffed a rolled comic book deeper into the rear pocket of his jeans. The wheels on his Schwinn Trooper squealed like a tortured rodent. He looked ridiculous on the tiny bike. He'd lived in Neptune Park, in a trailer, so he probably hadn't been able to afford something appropriate for his age. He slowed near a barbed-wire fence materializing and then disappearing. The strands of barbed-wire were supported by wooden posts every ten feet. He got off the Schwinn and sidled up to the strobing fence like a cowboy with six-shooters on his belt. He said, "You think you're bad?" to someone or something Emily couldn't see. The fence and wooden posts exploded and the invisible something knocked him to the road and stomped dents into his small body until he stopped moving. She couldn't see the bull, but the animal's wild grunts and hollers echoed across time. Then Donny Gross stood—bruised, bloodied, pieces of bone poking from his chest and his limbs. He picked up his bicycle and rode back into the darkness. As with Hop Robbins' wife, he returned, again and again, to challenge the invisible bull and to have his challenge violently answered.

The desire to help the boy, who should have been the same age as Emily, overcame her. He should not have died the way he did. The next time Donny Gross wheeled up on his Schwinn, he looked at her. He opened his arms. He groaned like an old man lifting something heavy. She battled what felt like a seventy-mile an hour wind to turn herself around and continue to the high school.

What a terrible, scary buzz! She assumed Jessica hadn't lied to her, that it would be over in an hour. People who'd written about the experience on the Internet said when the drug wore off, they swooshed back into their bodies and woke up in the normal world. She had no idea how much time she'd already spent under the influence. She breezed onto Seventh Street and glided toward Haggard High. She ignored young people flopping dead in the street, no doubt having been hit by invisible cars. When she reached the school, she floated through the building, through the chemistry labs on the first floor. She dripped between stacks of books in the library. And then she slowed as she emerged from the other side into the larger parking lot, just beyond the football field.

Years of bands playing the Haggard fight song, students cheering, plastic shoulder pads and helmets colliding, wove together to create a swooping cacophony she rode like a wave to the twenty-yard line. She hovered over the stands, near her seat at homecoming. Out of the darkness, Travis Agnew, stringy but strong, legs moving like a blur, leapt into the air to catch an invisible football. Then he dropped to the Earth, his body twisting and folding.

Emily froze, as she had the night of the game. On the field, Travis took to his feet, his mangled body forcing him to prop up his left side with both hands. He shuffled into the darkness and emerged once more, healthy, intact, only to fly to the heavens and be creased by the invisible defenders again.

She couldn't stand it. If helping Travis find peace meant taking his place, taking those hits for him for the rest of eternity, so be it. She felt useful, as though she had a purpose beyond looking good and earning A's in school. She drifted onto the field with no resistance. Travis ran straight at her, then slowed. He opened his arms and Emily flew into them without thinking anything but how wonderful to be with him again. The hunger morphed into the ticklish sensation she got on the first hill of a roller coaster.

She blinked and woke up in her room, on her bed. An invisible hand forced something under her tongue. It tingled for a moment, then her heart beat fast, faster, *too* fast. Pain shot through her chest.

The invisible hand shoved the white tablet under her tongue once more. Purple shadows of the living blurred around her. Her mother shook her finger at Kale and Jessica, her father spoke into his cell phone. Her heart beat too fast, the pain returned, and she closed and opened her eyes. This happened over and over as more people in the material world arrived—paramedics, Father Branch from St. Bridget's, the police. She watched her body hoisted onto a stretcher. The activity around her simmered. The room emptied. The walls of the house appeared and disappeared. She lost track of time, soon forgot the very concept. For a brief period, she wanted to resist the hand feeding her the tablet. Eventually, however, even that silly idea vanished.

THE BRIDGE

Almost four in the morning. Why the hell was he standing at the edge of a ravine in Raw Creek, Indiana? A stupid stunt to make peace with Laura, his seventeen-year-old daughter. Damn Sheila for pushing the girl on him at her most difficult age. He hadn't really been there the last six years of her life. She reminded him every day—"You think you can just say 'sorry' and it's all good?" Didn't matter the divorce had been Sheila's idea. The judge had given her custody and she didn't mind until her second marriage collapsed and she "needed space." What about *his* needs? He'd finally gotten himself in shape, ready to head out into the adventurous world of middle-aged dating. Now he had his kids at home, keeping him from meeting women at the Friday night St. Bridget's singles dance. Laura didn't care. He'd ask her to babysit her younger sister and she'd tell him she was meeting friends. "Vanessa's not my problem," she'd say. "Why don't you call Mom?"

"Sweetheart," he'd say, feeling stupid for pleading with a child, "your mother is…finding herself. I don't even know what that means. Probably something she read in a magazine. We got to take care of each other until she comes back from Turkey, or Greece, or wherever the hell she's gone to."

She refused to call him Dad—"Mom's in Morocco, Darrell. You know that."

And he'd give in. He'd stay home and watch Disney DVDs with Vanessa, who still loved him unconditionally. She'd just turned seven, as she liked to tell folks anytime he took her to a burger joint or the Walmart in Lublin. She sang to herself in the car, in her room drawing pictures on a sketchpad, or in the bathroom while she brushed her teeth. Every night at the dinner table, she asked him about his day at work. An absolute angel. He called her Little Miss Redemption. She liked to be tucked into bed before sleeping. She liked it when he read her Ramona books or took her to the movies. Despite her mother having purchased a smartphone for her when she was four, she found little use for it and often left it under a pile of clothes on the floor. She'd taught him how to comb her hair in the morning and put it in pigtails the way she preferred. She showed him how to construct the perfect peanut butter and jelly sandwich for her lunchbox. Anytime his students crawled under his skin and made him want to open the windows in his classroom and toss them out, he thought of Vanessa. Instant calm. *Little Miss Redemption.*

Laura, on the other hand, had barely spoken with him since moving in to his apartment. She spent most of her time at the mall in Merrillville. He'd seen her there once. He'd been shopping for a new battery for his laptop. He watched her lounging in a round near the food court with her friends, all focused on their individual phones. When she did come home, she went straight to her room. If she agreed to eat dinner, she'd sit at the table wearing earbuds, listening to mono-rhythmic noise loud enough for the rest of the world to hear.

Earlier that week, he'd entered her room without her permission. She was reading something on the Internet. Paragraphs of text. The idea of her deciphering something longer than a "tweet" thrilled him. "What you looking at?" he said. She told him about Raw Creek, a small town ten miles south of Bloomington. A dirt road called Cooley Avenue stopped at the edge of a ravine. The forest on the other side had a reputation of being so haunted locals never entered it. She said a covered bridge had once connected the road to the forest, but it collapsed while a woman crossed it to meet her lover. Classic ghost story material. He'd rolled his eyes.

"You think it's so funny, Darrell," she said, "go on down there and see for yourself."

He played along—"See what?"

She said, "You park your car at the edge of the ravine. Just after four in the morning, a woman opens the back door and gets in behind you. You don't look at her, you don't talk to her, you act like she ain't even there. Once she's in, the bridge appears. You put the car in neutral and it rolls across on its own."

He laughed. "Sweetheart," he said, "if that were true, I'd know of it." He taught history and his specialty was Indiana. He'd never read anything about a haunted bridge in Raw Creek.

"I've studied up on this, Darrell. It's all over the Internet."

He apologized and let her finish.

"On the other side, she gets out of the car and you put it in reverse and roll back across. Again, don't look at her, don't speak to her. Turn around while you're headed back. If you do everything right, as soon as you return to the other side, the bridge will disappear."

Again, he made the mistake of showing interest—"And if you screw it up?"

"You get her fixed on you," she said, "she'll take something from you. Something real valuable."

"Sounds serious."

"It's no joke, Darrell," she said. "People who've done it and messed up, they said the door closed when the woman got out and they were back on the other side of the ravine, without driving in reverse across the bridge."

"Well, that's incredible." He wanted to change the subject.

"You don't believe it?" she'd said. "You think I'm stupid?"

"Sweetheart…"

"Get lost." She said she hated him. Nothing new. He moped to the door, a sick feeling in his stomach, like fried food twisting his insides. Then he stopped.

"I know these things are important to you," he said.

"Doubt it."

The smell of perfume and hair spray filled the air in her room. Posters of singers, young men who looked as fragile as Faberge eggs, covered her walls. He asked her what he could do to demonstrate he cared about her, cared about her feelings, her interests. He figured she'd suggest buying her tickets to a concert or something.

"Take me to Raw Creek." Anticipation washed over her face like someone on the verge of finding God. "Can you do that, Dad? I want to see the bridge."

He said he'd think about it. Her wide, hopeful eyes dimmed. She jammed her pink buds into her ears and waved him off.

He'd spent the next day at school debating whether he should give in to the silly request. He'd studied urban folklore in college. The idea of putting a local myth to the test fascinated him. By the time his fifth period seventh graders rumbled into the classroom, fresh with energy from lunch and ready to raise hell, he'd become obsessed. Here would be an opportunity to sit in a car for five hours and force his daughter to get to know him better. "Let's leave the smartphone and earbuds at home, shall we?" he'd tell her. He could fly his skepticism about ghosts and other nonsense under the radar, demonstrate he understood the world better than she did, and maybe, just maybe, she'd take him seriously as a father.

That night, he did his own research. There were videos on *YouTube* of teenagers sitting in darkness, waiting for the woman and the bridge and encountering nothing. Had his daughter seen them? Looking further into the matter, he found chat boards with testimonies from people claiming to have gone through with the ritual, or whatever it was, and having returned with dreadful consequences. They'd made the mistake of glancing at the woman in the rearview mirror. Most of them described her as pale with stringy, black hair. This reinforced his skepticism. The ghost, as it were, seemed to have been inspired by Asian horror films and their American imitators. One theory cast her as a child who'd been fishing on the bridge when it collapsed. She'd fled for the other side but, obviously, didn't make it. Why four in the morning, then? What kind of child went fishing that early? Another said she'd been abused at home, had decided to run away and a tornado had splintered the bridge as she crossed it. The most recent theories involved a woman in her twenties who'd taken up an affair with a married man. She'd meet him just before dawn every morning in the forest. Mother nature intervened once more, this time with a bolt of lightning.

Those who claimed to have made eye contact or spoken with the woman said things didn't "feel right" afterward. They ended up on the other side of the ravine without actually driving back across the phantom bridge, just as Laura had said would happen. They promised to keep people updated, but never returned to the chat board. Unable to reconcile the differences between the articulate, written accounts and the goofy, booze and weed-laden videos, Darrell decided it best to investigate it, initially, on his own. If it were as benign as he suspected, he would take Laura there the next night.

He waited until the weekend. Friday. He could spend Saturday recuperating. He left just after eleven. Checked on Vanessa. Laura had been out with friends and returned, angry that she had to be at home. "You want to go to Raw Creek tomorrow," he said, "I need you here tonight, making sure Vanessa is okay." She argued that her sister was already asleep. He said, "We can skip this trip all together, if you like." She stuffed her buds into her ears and turned her back to him.

He cruised down I-65 with a half moon painting the rolling farmlands an electric blue. The highway remained empty, for the most part, with the exception of the jog through Indianapolis. He drove another sixty minutes, past Columbus and Bloomington, before getting off at the Raw Creek exit. Neither his GPS nor any map sites on the Internet recognized a Cooley Avenue. He had to stop at a twenty-four-hour Shell station just off the highway to ask. The attendant, a teenager who took his time removing his eyes from his smartphone, spoke to him through bulletproof glass. He tossed his bangs to the side of his head and said, "Yeah?" as though his attention were no less valuable than an ancient Pharaoh's. Darrell asked him if he knew how to get to the haunted bridge. The kid smirked.

"You going to hang with Gerty?"

Darrell must have looked confused.

"Gerty's the girl," said the attendant. "See that road there?" He pointed to a street running along the other side of the station.

"Take that about a mile. Houses'll start disappearing on you. That's how you know you're close. Put your brights on. You'll come up on a dirt road that's got a busted fence on both sides. That's your ticket, buddy. Just follow it until it stops. Like I said, keep those brights on. You don't want to roll into the ditch."

Darrell thanked him.

"And buddy," said the attendant, "she decides to ride with you, keep your eyes out of that rearview. You don't want her taking nothing from you, you hear me?"

He thanked the attendant again, not sure how to react to his last comment, and got back into his car.

As the ranch-style houses gave way to barren fields, he flipped on his high beams. Early morning mist rose off the undisciplined pavement. He veered left onto a road flanked by jagged posts with sagging barbed wire. Dirt and gravel crunched under his tires as he approached the ravine. He slowed and put the car in park a few yards shy of the edge. He left his brights on and stepped out to peer over the side. Trees and shrubs filled in the valley below. Maybe it had once been a river or possibly the creek the town was named after. Rotting planks of white and burgundy wood poked from the foliage. They pointed, like fingers, to the forest across the gorge.

None of the usual sounds of the night surrounded him—no crickets, no small animals moving through the grass. Aside from his idling Honda, there was only silence. The air chilled him and the mist swirled around his feet. He wondered, right then, what the hell he was doing there.

He hustled back to his car and turned off the lights. He wanted to sleep. He hadn't stayed up past midnight in years. The clock on the radio read 3:59. How absurd to have wasted gas driving down there. The numbers turned to 4:00 and he held his breath. Nothing happened. "Well, so much for that." He grabbed the gearshift, ready to put the car in reverse.

Light footsteps snapping twigs on the ground approached from the passenger side. The back door opened. Someone plopped down on the seat behind him. The door closed. He ground his teeth and fought the urge to look in the rearview mirror. Without thinking about it, he shifted to neutral. The car rolled forward. He put his hands on the steering wheel. A burgundy covered bridge with white trim materialized. The wheels banged a steady thump-thump-thump over the floorboards. He'd expected the woman, or whatever was in the car with him, to make some strange noise. He imagined a ghost from an Asian horror movie, dripping wet, maybe wheezing. As these thoughts tip-toed through his mind, he noticed the thing behind him had begun to breathe loudly. It *knew* he was thinking about it. He forced himself to picture Ms. Hunt, an algebra teacher at Haggard Middle School he'd wanted to go out with but had never found the guts to ask. She always wore a high-cut, light purple dress on casual Fridays. Her thighs had been hand-crafted by God. The eighth-grade boys called her a *fold*. He'd learned from the Internet that had replaced the term *milf* in these tender, more polite times. The breathing behind him got louder, anxious, desperate. Better to think of something pure—his daughters. He saw Laura, angry scowl on her face, brooding all the time. No good. Wasn't it her fault he was here? Better to think of Vanessa. How thrilled she'd been the first time he picked her up for his visitation weekend after she'd started kindergarten. Her mother had dressed her in Osh-Kosh overalls covered with red flowers and yellow butterflies. She sang "The Itsy-Bitsy Spider" every time she visited, when her mother still had custody. She hadn't sung it since moving in with him, preferring, instead, pop songs her sister liked. The thing in the back seat crooned in a hushed, raspy voice, *"The itsy-bitsy spider crawled up the water spout…"*

He wanted to turn around and smack it. They were close to the other side now. The headlights on his car opened up the forest. Massive Birch trees and Sycamores huddled together. Their skinnier branches resembled fingers, arched to grab anyone who got too close. The car stopped on its own. He waited for the thing behind him to leave. But it didn't. It just kept singing, *"…down came the rain and washed the spider out…"*

Why won't you get lost? He clenched his lips so he wouldn't say it out loud. He closed his eyes, thinking that would calm him. Was it playing a game with him? Taunting him? What the hell was taking it so damn long? He accidently opened his eyes, staring directly into the rearview mirror.

The woman's lovely blond hair spilled around the shoulders of her summer blue dress. She glared at him, her mouth open, her face in shock, as though he'd done something terrible to her. She got out and slammed the door. The bridge vanished. Darrell's car had returned to the other side of the ravine as though it had never moved at all.

"Dammit." He tried to convince himself it had been a hallucination. He'd investigated it so much his mind had put on a show. Maybe he'd fallen asleep and dreamt it. As he drove to the highway, he couldn't shake the feeling that somehow, in some way, the woman had stayed with him. He checked the rearview mirror, expecting to catch her staring at him. He wanted to get back to Haggard, as though that would somehow prevent any tragedy he'd invited. What did they mean, on the Internet, when they said the woman would take something valuable? His life? He'd just turned forty. His colleagues ribbed him, called him a fossil. Didn't seem so old now. He remembered all the plans he'd made—to write a book about Indiana's role in the Civil War. He'd wanted to go to Europe, something he hadn't been able to afford thanks to his wife and kids. He imagined his daughters growing up from here on without their father. His foot constantly smashed the pedal to the floor, sent his Honda rocketing over eighty miles an hour, before he'd realize this might be how the woman got him—a car accident. Convenient. Nobody would know what really happened. *Jesus...* He could see his daughters at his funeral. Laura, chewing gum and looking at her phone while Vanessa, God bless her, cried her little eyes out.

He roared into the parking lot next to his building, hopped out of his car, and ran up the steps to his apartment. His hands shook as he maneuvered his key into the bolt lock on his front door and whipped it open. He nearly fell into Laura's bedroom. She'd passed out wearing clothes she'd had on the night before. Her earbuds were still in her ears despite the blank screen on her smartphone. He shook her shoulders. "Laura, Laura, sweetheart, wake up, please."

She took a breath and rolled away from him.

"Laura," he said, "Sweetheart, I know things haven't been great, but please, please know that I love you, even if that doesn't mean anything to you now."

She slapped his hand. "Oh my God," she said, "you woke me up for *that*?"

He sat next to her, refused to move, until he heard his youngest child.

Vanessa, Little Miss Redemption, greeted her Saturday morning with music. She'd understand. She'd be happy to see him. He started down the hallway toward her room. And then he stopped. Two voices, Vanessa's and a breathy, raspy woman's, carried through her door, in unison, *"The itsy-bitsy spider crawled up the water spout..."*

BROKE

Serena noticed the window the first night they slept in the new apartment. She'd been brushing her teeth, hoping Jordan wouldn't be too tired to fool around. He still hadn't put together the bed frame. They'd be close to the floor, which was a little nasty since the property manager hadn't replaced the carpet. Twice she'd picked fingernail clippings from previous owners off the bottom of her bare feet. She'd have worn her slippers, but they were still packed away in one of the boxes in the living room. The move had been so sudden, out of necessity. Her conscience had compelled her to withhold evidence in discovery. The prosecutor's office fired her, agreed not to submit her situation to the state for further review. Was it fair? Of course not. She resisted the urge to call her boss a bigot. She couldn't shake the suspicion, though. She'd never seen Charlie Binder get in trouble for anything despite his constant incompetence. She doubted he'd be eighty-sixed without due process. She couldn't even fight it, knowing the outcome would be bad whether she won or lost. And now she and her husband had to rely on the ten dollars an hour he earned as an armed security guard at First Federal in Merrillville.

She called to him again. "You got to see this."

He moved through the dark hallway from their bedroom at a slug's pace, slender and wavy, like a stoned salamander on its hind legs. Before entering the tiny bathroom, he stuffed both hands into the back of his striped shorts and scratched his ass. "What's going on?" His eyes drooped the way they did anytime he'd worked too hard. He'd spent the day lugging boxes from the U-Haul to the apartment. "I ain't paying an extra day on this truck," he'd said, hustling up and down the front walk, looking like Atlas in the beginning and, by the end, the Lorax, hunched over and sweating like a pig.

"You see this?" She pointed to the only window in the bathroom.

Jordan put his hand on his forehead and sighed. "I told you I'd scrape all the frames and repaint them once we get settled."

Sometimes she could just scream, sharing oxygen with a man as sensitive as a brick wall. "You don't see anything unusual?" She traced her finger around the window, as though she were showing it off, like a model on *The Price is Right*.

He sat on the toilet ring. "Is this one of them tests? Are you testing me?"

"What time is it, Jordan?"

"Late." He picked behind his ear.

"It's almost midnight."

"Sure feels like it." He dropped his palms on his knees, made a smacking sound he probably hoped would end the conversation.

"Let me ask you this," she said. "Should the sun be shining through this window at eleven-thirty at night?"

The dummy finally looked over. Serena allowed him a moment to react. Jordan expected the world to make sense. His father had preached the gospel of hard work, suffering, and death. Anything inexplicable should either be ignored or attributed to the mysterious workings of Jesus. "Interesting." He stood and walked toward the window the way one might approach a wild animal. He reached for the latch on the top.

"Wait a minute," she said. "We don't know what this is." She hadn't been so quick to notice it herself. She'd been brushing her teeth, glancing between the mirror over the sink and the window. For a moment, her mind had convinced her it was still daytime. She peered through it, expecting to see the dead oak, crooked as an old man, on the side of the building. But there was only a pale blaze. She'd gone to the living/dining room, toothbrush in her mouth, toothpaste foaming on her tongue. The windows there and in the kitchen were dark, as they should have been. She'd returned to the bathroom, gawked a moment longer, and called Jordan over to take a look.

He said not to worry. "Trick of the light. Bet you anything." The latch gave some resistance, but eventually squealed as he pulled it open. Paint around the bottom chipped and flew off as he inched the window upwards. Instead of darkness waiting on the other side, a deep, orange glare poured into the room.

Serena stepped back. "This is freaky," she said. "Landlord's going to have to explain this." She tapped Jordan on his chest. "Don't unpack those boxes just yet. We may be moving."

"I don't think so." He snapped his neck when he spoke, like a hoodrat on *Jerry Springer*. "Let's see what's going on." He knelt by the window and squinted. "Is there a furnace room over here?"

How could he be so dense? They'd rented a corner apartment. There should have been nothing but brown grass, the dead oak, and shitty cars in the parking lot just past the crumbling sidewalk. He stuck his hand through the window without warning her. It *disappeared*.

"Interesting." He pulled his arm back into the bathroom, turned it up and down, appraising it like a diamond. "That is messed up." He jammed his hand out the window again, into the orange light, this time farther.

"Jordan," said Serena, "we don't need to be fooling with this."

He brought his hand back, examined it, and shrugged. Then, he poked his head through the window. For a moment, everything from the neck up vanished. Serena thought of a Frankenstein movie she'd seen where they showed a body after a guillotine had decapitated it.

But he returned, intact and wide-eyed. "Whoa," he said. "You got to see this."

"No," she said. "No way."

"Like another dimension," he said. "Like some shit you'd see on *Twilight Zone*." He opened the window farther.

"Jordan?"

He slammed his palms on the bottom of the frame, nudging it. White and yellow paint chips flaked off with each hit. A line formed on the sill and the floor underneath it. "Looks just like the outside, during the day, you know?" he said. "Except the air is the color of a tomato, and the sky, I swear, it's like a deep, deep purple. Like bubblegum purple."

"Whatever it is, baby, it's not right."

"Step aside." He put his hand on her thigh and shoved her toward the toilet. "I'm going to see what's what."

Her throat had gone dry. Jordan's curiosity had always been a comfort. Most things about him, in fact, had been in sync with what she decided she'd marry before she was graduated from law school. The geeks at Notre Dame did their best to thrill her, but they were missing something, something she might call *common sense*. They could tell her the minute details of Griggs vs. Duke Power, but if her car broke down, not one of them could look at the engine and surmise the problem. She'd hoped to start a family, live in a house somewhere between Indiana and Cleveland, where she'd grown up. She'd pictured the man she would wed tinkering with a lawnmower on a Saturday afternoon. Then she met Jordan at the bank. He'd walked straight up and said he wanted to chill with her. No games. No bullshit. He didn't talk law shop, he didn't speak the liberal arts gibberish she'd been indoctrinated with as an undergrad at Ohio State. Sometimes, though, Jordan's desire to look deeper into simple things could be a problem. Like when he'd taken apart her phone to fix a glitch with the headphone jack. After he'd put it back together, it got stuck on a weather app. She'd turn it off and on and every time it'd go right to telling her the temperature outside and nothing else. She had to buy a new phone, get a new number. A real pain in the ass.

Jordan climbed through the window, got stuck for a moment, his legs dangling over the windowsill, like the bottom half of a mannequin, suspended in the air. She heard him cuss as he wiggled the rest of the way. His entire body disappeared. She wanted to call 911 as soon as his foot disintegrated in the orange light. She put down the lid on the toilet, sat on it, and waited. The legal possibilities troubled her—*Your honor, he disappeared into another dimension. At least, he called it another dimension.* Surely she'd be able to show the police the window, how it projected sunlight at night, how, upon opening it, an entirely different atmosphere drifted in. She dozed off, resting her head in her hand on the dirty sink.

Jordan made a mess of noise as he crawled back into the bathroom. He tumbled onto the cracked tiles on the floor. "Dammit," he said. He stood and brushed paint chips and dust and ceramic flakes off his legs. "That's some weird shit, let me tell you."

"What the hell took you so long?" Serena examined him, expected him to somehow be different, replaced by a pod or something. But he looked normal, just a little dirty. She couldn't believe he'd actually gone out the window in his boxers.

"Nice try," he said. "Wasn't even gone a minute."

She pointed to the alarm clock on the floor in their bedroom. "It's one in the morning. It wasn't even midnight when you left." She pointed at it again, then forgot everything she'd meant to say. "Oh...*shit.*"

Dark bluish hints of night showed on the other side of the window. The rising trunk of the dead oak interrupted her view of the parking lot and the broken streetlamps, failing to watch over it.

"Well," said Jordan, "there you go."

"What do you mean?" She wanted to call scientists, paranormal investigators, those people on TV who got excited by every bump and scratch they heard in abandoned houses, somebody, anybody who could explain what the hell had happened.

"The shit was broke," he said. "I fixed it."

She woke up grumpy. Jordan had gone straight to sleep after the incident with the window. Ever since she'd been fired, he always claimed to be exhausted. They'd made love the night she came home and told him the bad news. He hadn't put a good hand on her since. "I've been on my feet all day," he'd say. "You expect me to be on point now? I'm a working man, baby." Bad enough he wouldn't even wrap his arm around her, let her know he was still on her team. He'd hogged more than half of the quilt and, on top of all that, the mattress had gotten thin and she could feel bumps in the floor underneath it. Like sleeping on a gravel road. First thing she said when he finally rolled out of bed was, "You going to put the frame together? Last night was like camping. You know I don't like camping, Jordan."

"Yeah, all right." He didn't look at her, he just stood, jammed his hands down his boxers, and scratched himself all the way to the toilet. She went into the kitchen to start breakfast. She found the pots and pans in a Gerber's box they'd swiped from a shopping cart at Walmart. They'd bought eggs and a loaf of bread after returning the U-Haul. "Dammit," she said. They'd forgotten butter. Well, whatever. She pulled the toaster from a box on the counter and plugged it in. Grime filled the cracks in the wall socket's frame. She washed her hands after dropping in two pieces of bread. She started the stove and slid the skillet on the front burner. The eggs were from a Family Express convenience store. Generic. They crumbled when she cracked them on the side of the pan. She fished shell fragments from the sizzling whites near the edge.

The toast popped out black and flaking. She dug through a Pampers box for the salt and peppershakers. She twisted the pepper grinder over the pan, then she salted the eggs. Normally, she'd have cooked them on medium, but she left the burner on high. They needed to finish so she could cover up the bread before Jordan stumbled in, looking for another excuse to complain.

He stood in the doorway. "Damn," he said. "We can't even afford the morning paper no more. Don't know how I'm going to get my Zen on, I can't read the sports page."

So much for a peaceful breakfast.

"I'll figure something out." She nodded at the folding card table they'd placed by a window in the living/dining room. "Take a seat. I got breakfast."

For whatever reason, he stood still for another minute. He moved his tongue around the front of his teeth with his mouth closed—his go-to gesture when he thought he'd made a point. Finally, he strolled toward the table, swerving like he was some kind of OG, walking up on a rival.

She shoved a spatula under the two eggs she'd fried for him. Stubborn as hell without any grease or butter on the pan. One of the yokes broke as she floated them to the burnt toast she'd set on a paper plate. She placed the eggs so they drooped over the sides of the bread. "Come get your food, baby," she said. She peeled her lone egg off the pan and put it in the center of the black circle on her toast. She set her paper plate on the table and sat on a box filled with textbooks she'd kept from college.

Jordan took two bites. He lifted the eggs off his bread. "What's up with this toast, woman?" He picked at it with his fork. "Shit's burnt straight through."

She spoke with her mouth full. "You know that thing's got a mind of its own."

He glared at her, then at the toaster on the counter. "All right, then." He got up with his plate and placed it next to the stove. He took the toaster into his hands and shook it. "Bread in the fridge?"

"Where else would it be?"

He took out the bag, knocked a piece of bread into his hand and put it into one of the two slots on the toaster. "We're going to figure this out." The heat level indicator on the bottom of the side had been set to medium. He nudged it closer to the lighter end and pressed the lever down to cook the bread.

"We've been through this before," she said. The dummy's eggs would get cold and he'd bitch and moan about making new ones, about wasting food even though he was the fool doing all the wasting. "Just eat your breakfast."

The toast popped out with a stream of smoke. The entire piece of bread had been charred. Serena covered her mouth to stifle a laugh.

Jordan pushed the heat lever in the opposite direction.

"Oh, okay," she said. "So you're just going to go through a whole loaf like that? Don't get shitty with me when you have to go shopping tonight and buy a new one."

The next piece of bread shot out darker than the previous. The kitchen filled with smoke. He turned the toaster upside down and smacked it. "Wouldn't be a problem," he said, "if both of us were still bringing in a paycheck."

She threw her fork on the table. "Really? You're going to hit me with this? *Now?*"

He opened the bottom of the toaster and dumped the crumbs onto the counter. "I ain't going to step on you for protecting an innocent man. I get that." He pulled the plug from the socket in the wall. "I still don't understand why you don't sue, seeing as how you know for a fact they wouldn't treat dumbass Charlie Binder the same. This ain't 1819, know what I'm saying? We're in the twenty-first century and we're still getting sold down the river?"

How many times would she be asked to explain? "I told you," she said, "I might win the battle, but I'll lose the war. I take them to court, they'll sabotage any chance I have of ever practicing again."

"Sounds like bullshit to me." He found the box with silverware in it and stirred up a racket, rummaging through the utensils. He pulled out a butter knife and used it to unscrew the bottom of the toaster.

"What are you doing?" She turned herself to keep a full eye on him.

The screws fell onto the counter. "I'm going to fix this, baby," he said. "I can't fix much, what's going on these days, you know, us, and such, I can't fix it all. But goddamn if I'm not going to take a stab at fixing this damn toaster."

She knew he'd gone past the point of no return. Still, she thought she might be able to talk him into putting the toaster together again before he caused irreparable damage. "How long have we been eating shitty bread? Don't see why it's such a big deal this morning."

He put his hands on his hips. For one crazy moment, he reminded her of her mother, who'd always felt the need to correct the manners of everyone except for herself. He said, "It's offensive, Serena. Eating charred up toast is *offensive*." Then he jammed the butter knife into the heart of the machine and wedged out the coils. They spilled onto the counter with tiny 'boing' noises and rolled back and forth between the screws. He stabbed at the insides like Jack the Ripper. Metal and plastic pieces bounced off the surface of the counter like hard drops of rain on a sidewalk.

"Guess we won't be having toast for a while," she said.

He examined the hollow toaster, shrugged, and then attached the bottom to it and twisted the screws back in. He turned it right side up and plugged it in. Then he placed two slices of bread into the slots and pressed down on the lift carriage.

Serena held her hand over her mouth. She didn't want to insult him. Tears formed at the corners of her eyes as she struggled to keep herself from laughing.

"You ain't going to think it's that funny in a minute." He leaned on the counter and stared at the lifeless toaster with the beaming eyes of a father watching his child takes its first steps.

She crossed her legs and her arms. She wished she'd brought her smartphone to the kitchen. Filming her husband, at that moment, could have launched a *YouTube* channel and put an end to her need to find a new job.

She listened to the morning birds outside. A light wind danced around the building, occasionally rattled the windows in the apartment. Finally, Jordan took both pieces of bread out of the toaster and held them in front of Serena's face like a card player showing aces. "What did I tell you?"

She took her hand away from her mouth. "Seriously?"

"They burnt?"

Again, with a little more force, she said, "Seriously?"

"They ain't burnt, right?"

Raising her arms, demonstrating a slight retreat, she said, "Your honor, I cannot argue."

"There you go." He tossed the floppy, uncooked bread onto her plate, on top of her food. "I fixed it."

She spent the afternoon unpacking her clothes and makeup and loading the dressers built into their bedroom. The wooden drawers were rotting and newspapers lining them had gotten stuck to the bottoms. She washed them out. Tried to remove the newspapers, but the glue underneath refused to let go.

For lunch, she ordered a sandwich from Houck's Deli. She discarded the bag and wrapper in the dumpster outside so Jordan wouldn't know she'd spent money. Afterward, she continued work on her resume. Would her former boss keep his word, not tell any potential employers what she'd done? Like she was the first assistant district attorney to bury prior convictions. In this case, the defendant, a foreman at Liberty Steel in Gary, had punched a police officer during a traffic stop. The guy was lucky to be alive.

Most cops would have shot him. The man hadn't done anything but ask why he'd been pulled over. She'd found an assault charge from twenty years ago in South Los Angeles. Her boss reminded her, just before he fired her, that any evidence could be inflated in court. At the very least, it would have given the public defender something else to worry about.

Perhaps she could apply for a civil rights outfit. The pay wouldn't be nearly as good, but they'd understand her compassion. They'd welcome it, in fact. She sketched her week, planned to go to the Lublin Public Library and use their Internet to start sending out resumes and cover letters.

Feeling as though she'd accomplished something, she plugged in their television and attached a digital antenna she'd picked up at Walmart. Jordan would ask her what she'd done with her day, like him making minimum wage while she earned nothing gave him the right to talk to her like he was her father. She'd tell him her plan and, hopefully, he'd assemble their bedframe and leave her the hell alone. She fiddled with the antenna, found Channel 9, out of Chicago. The Bulls were beating the Pacers in an early game. The players kept breaking into pixels and the sound constantly tripped over itself. She placed her beanbag chair she normally read in next to the TV and held the antenna in one hand until the signal settled. A little troublesome, but she didn't care. She dozed for most of the fourth quarter. Jordan's big, clumsy feet stamping in the front hall brought her to full attention.

He stood in the doorway to the living/dining room, in his beige and brown security guard uniform, staring at the television. Serena had dropped the antenna somewhere during her nap. The evening news broadcast looked like an old 1980s video game as it dissolved into tiny blocks and then rearranged itself searching for a clean signal. And then it would start all over again.

"The hell's wrong with the picture?" he said.

She looked at the ceiling. *Dear Lord, don't start this.* She picked up the antenna and tilted it in her hand until the image on the television behaved. "It's nothing, baby."

He took off his gun belt and placed it on a space on the couch between boxes they hadn't unpacked. The Glock in the holster landed on the cushion with a soft thud. He walked closer to the television, then looked at Serena. "So you're just going to sit there like that, trying to watch TV and relax?"

"It's okay," she said. "We'll figure out a good place for the antenna once we have all the furniture settled."

"Let me see it." He snapped his fingers at the antenna.

She wanted to ask just who the hell he thought he was, ordering her like a dog. She handed it to him. "I wish you wouldn't fuss over it."

After standing on different sides of the television, holding the antenna at different angles, watching the picture and sound fragment into different patterns, he said, "It's broke." He put the antenna down on the floor and the television screen went black, save for a thin, pink line running through the middle.

"Maybe," she said. "We'll get a new antenna when we get a new toaster, how about that?"

"This wouldn't be happening if we still had cable." He gave her The Look, staring down at her like her father used to when she'd tell him she wanted to go to the movies with her friends on Sundays instead of church. Jordan rummaged through boxes in the kitchen. Metal clanged, heavy things fell onto the floor. He returned with a crowbar and a hammer.

She stared past him, at the open bathroom door. "Jordan?" she said. "What exactly did you see on the other side of that window last night?"

His shoulders flinched, as though she'd flicked his ear. "I told you, wasn't nothing special." He unscrewed the RF line connecting the antenna to the TV. "I walked to the tree, looked at the tomato and bubblegum sky, and came back." He unplugged the television. He picked up the crow bar and flipped it a couple of times, like a baseball player, checking his bat before stepping to the plate. "Doubt I was out there for more than a minute."

"You were gone for over an hour, remember?"

His mouth twisted and drew back. "You trying to sell me some revisionist shit?" He looked at her for a moment longer and shook his head. "I got to fix this television."

"It's the antenna, Jordan," she said. "The antenna's the problem."

"We'll see about that." He positioned the long end of the crowbar inside the seam running down the side of the TV screen. He picked up the hammer and beat the curly end of the crowbar until the plastic busted and the television split like an old CD case.

"Jordan!" She put her hands over her ears, as though that might reverse what had just happened. "What the hell is wrong with you?"

The television collapsed onto the floor. Its guts looked like a cheap computer, a few green circuit boards scattered across a miniature city of silver streets and corridors between tiny round and rectangular structures. Serena didn't know how any of it fit together. She'd have bet whatever she had left in her bank account Jordan didn't know either. He jammed the crowbar under a circuit board and pulled up until it snapped in two.

"Dammit, Jordan," she said. "Television is all I got when you're at work and I'm worn out from looking for a job. What the hell am I supposed to do now?"

He knelt and smashed the remaining circuit boards with the hammer. The TV screen cracked and shattered. Tiny bits of glass sparkled on the dirty, once-yellow carpet like iced-over snow. When he'd beaten absolutely anything he, for whatever reason, felt needed to be destroyed, he plugged in the television again and set the screen upright against the wall.

"You really showed it who's boss," she said.

He stuffed the hammer under his arm and walked by her, to the couch. He picked up the remote control, which had fallen into the space between the boxes and his gun belt. He pressed the 'on' button and smiled. "There you go," he said.

That was it. Something had gone wrong. He needed to see a doctor, see if, shit, she didn't know—something chemical, in the brain? Would they even be able to cure him? "You're sick, Jordan," she said. "No sane person would do that." She pointed at the mutilated television. "What you just did, what you did to the toaster this morning?"

His mouth turned upward, toward his ear. "Is the picture messing up?"

"Jordan…"

He stepped toward her, shoulders raised. "Is…the picture… messing…up?"

Folding her arms across her chest, she said, "Jordan, there's no picture at all."

"Then it's fixed." He started for the kitchen.

She said, "You're going to the doctor's, Jordan. There's something very off with you." She listened to him drop the tools onto the cheap, faded linoleum.

When he returned, he moved the boxes on the couch to the floor. He put his hand on his gun belt and said, "Let's watch some TV, baby."

"Where's my phone?" she said. "Let's see if we can't get you into urgent care."

Jordan unsnapped the small strap holding his company-issued Glock in the holster. "I told you to sit here and watch some TV with me."

"Jordan," she said, "the television is broken. There's nothing to watch."

He squinted, turned his head side to side. "So you're telling me you don't see anything on the screen?"

"That's right," she said. "I don't see a thing."

Rolling his tongue in front of his teeth, he looked her up and down. "So your eyes ain't working?" He pulled the gun from the holster. "Let's take a closer look, baby."

USEFUL THINGS

Penelope had seen the small, wooden table and insisted he retrieve it. Gideon called it trash. They'd walked along 8th Street every Sunday for over a year without noticing the gray building or the silver dumpster in the parking lot in front of it. Might have been private property. They could have been prosecuted. But he knew that wouldn't stop her. Half the furniture in their apartment had been found on the sidewalk, in alleys, and second-hand shops. It hadn't bothered him when they moved in together. At some point, though, he'd expected her to develop an interest in chairs that didn't have permanent pizza stains on them or cracked, missing backs or smelly couch cushions with cotton pluming from open wounds.

"We need it for the kitchen," she said. "I don't have enough room between the sink and the stove to cut veggies."

He sighed and stared at the featureless high-rise towering over them. The windows were opaque and reflected dull, autumn clouds. Were there cameras aimed at the lot? Security guards inside, waiting to pounce? Jesus, he wouldn't get home in time for the Bears game if he didn't do what she asked. She'd argue and cry and he'd have no choice. And if he refused outright, she'd pout and ruin the rest of the afternoon. She'd occupy the couch like a protester, giving him the silent treatment while he sat on the ratty recliner in their living room waving a digital antenna this way and that to keep the television signal from fragmenting.

He grabbed the top of the dumpster and hoisted himself to

a ledge created by the fork pockets. His right hand slipped on an orange, jelly-like substance someone had splashed across the lip. As suspected, the table was garbage—the legs had splintered beyond repair. He dropped to the ground and said, "Useless."

"What's the story?" she said.

"Super-glue and duct tape couldn't save it." He sniffed the orange gunk oozing between his fingers. Smelled like gasoline. "The hell is this?" His flesh itched like it had been poked with sewing needles. He wiped his hand on a clean side of the dumpster. "Probably some bold new hepatitis. Airborne, no less."

"Don't be neurotic," she said.

On the walk back to their apartment, he tried to put his arm around her, comfort her, knowing she'd really wanted the table. She refused him, however, insisting he wash up first.

In their cramped bathroom, filled with her stash of cleansers and make-up, he poured Dial on his palm. His skin tingled as the soap settled. He turned on the faucet and used one of her nailbrushes to grind in the soap. Satisfied he'd killed any possible contaminants, he changed the water to cold and then shook his hand dry. In the scant light provided by a flickering lamp over the mirror, it appeared as though he'd developed freckles where the substance had been.

He took a better look in the living room. Pink spots no bigger than the mouth of a straw decorated his palm. He showed them to Penelope, who had turned on the television to a British drama on PBS.

"Fascinating." She went back to watching her program.

"You don't sound concerned."

She sighed. "It's a rash, or something," she said. "If it doesn't fade in a couple of days, go see Dr. Fremde."

He sat in the plaid upholstered recliner she'd had him swipe from a sidewalk outside an apartment complex near the library. According to the clock on a VCR they'd purchased from a Salvation Army sale, the Bears game would start in twenty minutes.

"Where are we in this?" he said.

"Huh?"

"How much longer will this be on?" He pointed at the TV as though it were guilty of murder.

"I don't know." She propped her arm on the top of the couch. She scratched a scab on her knee, peeking from under a daisy-colored sundress she'd restored after finding it in a bin of rejected clothes at Goodwill.

He pulled the lever on the side of the recliner, letting the bent footrest swing out. The back of the chair lowered. He closed his eyes, hoping to grab a nap and some energy to stand his ground at one o'clock, when the game started.

He dozed off until three. The television channel had been changed to the Bears game. The second half had just kicked off. They were losing to a Green Bay team that had yet to win a contest all season. Of course. He should have known better. "Honey?" he said. He wanted to thank her for being considerate and leaving the TV on while he slept. He heard her loud, rough snores from their bedroom. He reached down to fold in the footrest so he could run to the kitchen for a can of Schlitz. As he grabbed the wooden handle, however, he stopped.

The red spots on his palm had indented, as though someone had used a thumbtack to push them just enough to leave a mark. More disturbing, the itch he'd experienced when he first touched the gunk on the dumpster had spread to his wrist.

"Honey!" He bolted from the recliner and nearly knocked their bedroom door off its hinges. "Honey," he said, "holy shit and crap be all!"

She took her time opening her eyes. She breathed deeply and said, "Man, this better be good."

He knelt by the mattress they'd picked up at a garage sale for ten bucks. The fabric had torn at all four corners. He held his palm in the sunlight snaking through cracks in the blinds she'd found in a battered trashcan near a bail bonds office. Enough of the slats were bent or broken, they didn't do much to cover the windows. With his left hand, he pointed at the tiny craters in his skin. "Call me crazy, but this doesn't look right."

She squinted, rose to her elbows. When he brought his hand closer for her inspection, she said, "Good grief, get that out of my face!"

"And I think it's spreading." He turned his wrist sideways.

"Sweetheart," she said, "if it doesn't get better in two days, you see Dr. Fremde, you get some cream or antibiotics or whatever, and you go from there."

"What if it gets worse?"

"Then you know you're not wasting your money at the doctor's office." She pulled a *Transformers* quilt over her head. She'd snatched it from a pile of bedclothes behind a dormitory at Valpo. Through the fabric, she said, "Don't bug me again unless something falls off."

He woke from a dream in which his hand had turned into finished oak and termites had emerged from within, chewing their way through it. Penelope had already gotten up, taken care of her business on the toilet, and started her shower. He turned on a ceramic R2-D2 lamp on the nightstand next to his side of the bed. Both obtained, according to Penelope, for dirt cheap, at a garage sale in Pawpaw Grove.

The indented freckles had pushed so far into his skin his palm looked like a Martian landscape of smooth, deep craters. He ran his fingers from his left hand across the holes. Had he been a child, he would have found the sensation fascinating. He hopped out of bed, adjusting his loose boxers before they dropped to his ankles, and headed for the bathroom. Then he reconsidered. Penelope had been so dismissive. Would she tell him to put on some Band-Aids and stop being a whiner?

She stepped from the bathroom wrapped in a sturdy towel she'd purchased at an army surplus store. As she passed him, she kissed him on the cheek and said, "Morning."

She pulled wrinkled panties and a bra from a poorly repainted dresser she'd made him buy at an estate sale in Crown Point. The light blue and pink polka-dotted bra had a broken strap she'd fixed with a paper clip. She found a purple skirt and vanilla blouse in her closet and put herself together. She counseled students at

Ivy Tech and prided herself on her professionalism. When she noticed him staring at her, she said, "What?" She peeked at herself in a broken mirror they'd spotted in an alley next to a barbershop. "Not working?" she said, pointing to her outfit.

He raised his hand high enough for her to see the damage. She took his wrist and angled him toward a crooked, arced floor lamp by her side of the bed. "Make a fist," she said.

His fingers could barely curl before the skin around the holes closed like tiny mouths, squeezing his flesh and bones. "Dammit," he said, pulling away from her.

"You probably shouldn't drive." She dug through her purse and produced her cell. She dialed and waited. "Hey, it's me," she said into the phone. "I'm not going to make it in today." She listened, confirmed whatever her coworker had asked her, and hung up. She nodded at him and said, "Let's get you to the doctor's."

He sat in Dr. Fremde's waiting room, holding his infected hand, wishing he could read one of the *Sports Illustrated* magazines on the coffee table in the middle of the leather, u-shaped seats. Penelope flipped through a *Psychology Today*. Every now and then, she'd mutter, "What a load of shit." She turned to him and whispered, "None of these people have ever put their bullshit ideas to practical use, know what I'm saying?"

He nodded at the other patients in the other fancy chairs, reading other magazines. She held up the *Psychology Today*. "I'm talking about these theory junkies who never put their money where their gibberish is, you know?"

"I guess so." The holes in his palm had gotten deeper and wider. The bones in his hand ached, like an elephant had sat on them. Pink spots on his wrist had started to indent.

When the nurse called his name, he asked Penelope if she wanted to go with him. "You're a big boy," she said.

The nurse led him to a shiny, digital scale near an anti-smoking poster, weighed him, and then sat him down in a private room. Colorful portraits of the human body with no skin covered the walls, each illustrating different possible catastrophes. Beneath them were pamphlets explaining everything from hemorrhoids to dementia. "And what brings you here today?" she said.

He showed her his palm.

She waved her hand in front of her nose. "How'd that happen?"

He explained.

She said, "I think I'm just going to get Dr. Fremde."

The doctor arrived within a few minutes. He filled the doorway, being both tall and heavy. He carried a clipboard under his giant arm and a cup of coffee from a café called Le' Roasters. His thick, square-framed glasses rested on top of his bald scalp. "Susan says you've got a doozy." After examining Gideon's palm from a distance, the doctor put his coffee on a counter beneath a supply cabinet. He grabbed latex gloves from a dispenser over the sink. He twisted the infected hand. "That hurt?"

"Yes."

Running his gloved fingers over the holes in Gideon's palm, the doctor said, "Interesting." He asked if he had any idea what had caused the infection.

Gideon told him about the table and the dumpster and the orange gunk.

"Let's wrap that up," said the doctor, "make sure it doesn't collect any hitchhikers."

On the way home, they stopped at a newspaper bin and grabbed copies of *The Lake County Independent* and *The Haggard Caller*. Under normal circumstances, he'd have gone to the library and used a computer to search for jobs. He felt guilty, making Penelope lose a day of work when money was already slim. He would repay her by spending the evening with his nose buried in the classifieds.

The doctor had smeared his hand in cortisone and wrapped it tight with a cloth bandage. Gideon told him his arm had begun to tingle, the same as his palm and wrist. The doctor said if the holes got bigger, he should check himself into St. Mary's. When pressed, the doctor refused to say how serious he thought the situation might be.

As Gideon browsed construction jobs in the classifieds, desperate to find someone in need of a roofer, he imagined the worst possible scenario—amputation. He would be mutilated. The holes in his palm throbbed, dug deeper into the bones in his hand. He ignored the pain and focused on his lack of employment. Nobody, it seemed, needed a man with his own tools to lay tar and shingles in October. Of course.

Penelope suggested he broaden his search. "Maybe you can get a general labor gig, something easy." She said it as though it were possible. Too many people more qualified than he applied for those jobs. She wouldn't hear it. "Look," she said, "I understand you've got a situation and all, but let's think further down the road. We need money."

He scanned other categories—nanny jobs in Crown Point and Hammond, phone sex operators (*All Genders Welcome!*), endless trucker routes.

The bones in his hand cracked and blood splattered through the bandage. He fell out of the recliner and rolled on the floor. Penelope rushed over from the kitchen. She took off a *Betty Boop* apron she'd bought at Goodwill and threw it on the couch. "Let me see," she said.

"No." He clutched his hand to his chest. He didn't want to know what had happened.

She said, "Don't be a baby." She forced his wrist into her fingers and removed the bandage. "Oh God…"

The holes had busted through the other side. He held his good hand over the gushing wounds while Penelope ran to the bathroom. She returned with a stack of *Sesame Street* towels she'd nabbed at a going-out-of-business sale at a pre-school. She wrapped the wound once more. "Keep pressure on it," she said. Then she helped him put on his shoes.

Blood soaked through the towels and dripped onto the otherwise glossy white tiles in the reception area at St. Mary's. The nurse behind the desk, a thin woman with James Dean glasses and a tattoo of a spider web on her neck, walked them to a waiting area on the other side of two white, spotless automatic doors.

She told him to hop up onto a table behind a curtain and called for another nurse to attend to him. Penelope leaned against the wall. She chewed her fingernails.

The holes in his palm had gotten so big they had become one. He could see straight through his hand.

A nurse with three rings in her left nostril approached. She looked at his wound and flinched. "Let's get Dr. Metzger." Her canvas shoes swished in a quick rhythm across the polished floor. She came back with a round, Charlie Brown-faced doctor in green scrubs. His entire body shook, suggesting he'd had too much coffee, or cocaine, or both.

"Evening." The doctor glared at the hole in Gideon's hand. He asked if he'd been shot. Gideon told him the story. "Let's get an MRI and see what's going on." He spoke to him as though he might be a foreigner who only understood shouted English—"Are you in pain?"

Gideon said, "It's a full ten on the Richter scale."

The doctor instructed the nurse and disappeared.

Gideon turned his wrist around. The indented red spots had dug small holes into his flesh, like his palm that morning. He wanted to tell the nurse to cancel the MRI. No doubt about the next step. "Hey," he said to Penelope, almost whispering, "I'm scared."

A nurse with Conan the Barbarian and Sheena tattooed on his forearms wheeled over a wobbly metal cart. He prepared a syringe with morphine from a small, labeled bottle. "This'll keep you calm." He tied a rubber hose around Gideon's left bicep, tapped a vein to attention, and put the needle in him. Little feet raced through Gideon's bloodstream, their steps warm and relaxing. Before the nurse removed the syringe, Gideon's shoulders collapsed and a pleasant weight begged him to lean forward.

Penelope said she'd be with him for the operation. He asked her if she'd dump him, now that he'd be incomplete. She joked, maybe thinking a good laugh is what he needed. She said, "Long as they don't cut something else off."

When she followed him and the army of nurses prepping him into pre-op, they told her to wait in a room down the hall. "There's coffee and vending machines," they said.

They'd switched from morphine to a drug he'd never heard of once the decision to amputate had been made. They'd taken as close a look at his arm as possible, using the fanciest equipment Penelope's insurance would cover. Something they couldn't identify had gone to work on his flesh. They brought in two different specialists to discuss the infection. None of them had a clue. Dr. Metzger assured Gideon, "Last thing you want is this bugger taking any more real estate."

Nurses helped him change into a fresh gown. It smelled like the vinyl Darth Vader costume he'd worn five straight Halloweens as a kid. They led him by his good arm to a scale and weighed him. Many people spoke to him at the same time. Their voices jumbled, morphed into a cacophony. As he lay down on a new table, an anesthesiologist arrived. She spoke with a French accent. "I am Dr. Coucher," she said. "I will send you cheerfully into the horizon, no?" She prepared a large syringe with a yellow liquid and injected the drug through an IV they'd plugged into his good hand.

"I got to warn you," said Gideon, "stuff that's supposed to knock you out usually doesn't work on me."

Dr. Coucher laughed. "Okay, cowboy, we'll see what we can do." She produced what looked like an oxygen mask and placed it over his mouth. "Take a deep breath."

They'd moved him to a room full of groaning patients. He remembered where he was, why he was there. He glanced at his infected arm, couldn't find it in the dim lighting. He rolled over, thinking, if he put weight on it, he'd locate it. But he just wobbled to the side and back. The pressure on his shoulder produced a wave of pain across his chest. He felt for his right hand with his left, grabbed air, and realized the operation had taken place.

A nurse he couldn't see said, "This one's awake. Prepare a triple-dose of dilaudid." She whispered to him. "If you need to move your bowels, let us know so we can get a bedpan."

His eyes adjusted to the light. He craned his neck, searching for his missing arm. "This isn't real," he said.

Someone pumped his blood full of dilaudid and he allowed the drug to carry his mind away. When he came to, he assumed, he'd be at home. His palm, hand, wrist, and arm would be normal, where they were supposed to be, and everything that had happened since Sunday would turn out to be a very, very bad dream.

He sobered up to an orderly lumbering over him, pushing him in a large bed through the halls of St. Mary's. The man had a 1970s Afro and constantly said things like, "How you doing, chief?" and "Mind your feet, chief, we're rounding a corner." He stopped at an elevator wide enough to drive a car onto. He pushed the call button and stood by the door. "Whew," he said. "Can't wait for this night to be history."

Gideon wanted to say something, to be polite. His head spun from the remnants of the dope they'd given him over the last...how many hours had he been there? Was it Tuesday? Wednesday? He gawked at the massive bandage tied around his shoulder. Where the hell was his arm? "Oh God," he said.

"Don't you fret, chief," said the orderly. "Just a little shift in existence, nothing more."

The elevator arrived. The door rumbled open. The orderly pulled the bed from the other side and pushed a button for a higher floor. "They're going to set you in a nice room." He whistled a song Gideon had never heard, then he said, "You like satellite television? They got brand new TVs in these rooms. ESPN, Fox Sports, the NFL network. Everything you need to know, right there, at your convenience."

Cables slapped the walls outside the elevator. Gideon must have looked concerned. The orderly said, "She sounds troubled, but this old freight ain't ever let us down." When it stopped, the orderly pulled the bed out past him, pushing it on the side, before he stepped to the back again and wheeled it to a desk. He took a chart off the foot of the bed and showed it to an older nurse on duty. She scratched her brown and gray hair and typed something in a computer. "Five-seventeen," she said.

"All right then." As the orderly moved the bed into room 517, two nurses, large women laughing at a joke Gideon hadn't heard, joined them. They smelled like cigarette smoke. They worked with the orderly to hoist him onto a stationary bed. "All right, chief," said the orderly, "you just pretend you're in a luxury hotel."

One of the nurses checked the clipboard from the previous bed. The other hooked up a fresh IV drip. She said, "Dr. Metzger wants to keep you here a bit longer, make sure the infection's been headed off at the pass."

Gideon tried to grab his forehead. The IV prevented him from moving his free hand. He'd become useless. "I think I've got a headache," he said.

"No problem," said the nurse. "We'll get you something as soon as Dr. Metzger takes a look at you."

He heard Penelope's voice in the hallway. Nothing in his life had ever sounded so sweet and harmonious, so completely perfect for that precise moment. She entered the room. The nurses fussed with him, arranging tubes, showing him how to turn on the flat-screen television mounted on the wall, and explaining how to use the restroom so he didn't fudge his IV drip. Penelope said, "Can I see him?"

"Oh," said the nurse who'd been speaking with him, "is this your wife?"

He felt embarrassed, for the first time, saying, "No. Not yet."

Penelope hugged him, acted as though nothing were awkward about the lack of his right arm. He wanted to return the embrace, but couldn't. When she stood once more, she wiped her eyes. "I don't know why I was so nervous."

An unpleasant itch, the same itch he'd felt in his palm and his wrist, started in his shoulder and spread across his chest. It moved faster than before, as though his attempt to thwart it had *offended* it. He wanted to say to Penelope, "Don't let go." If she'd been upset during his operation, however, how would she feel once he told her the infection was on its way to his heart? Better to look strong, enjoy the nice, new television while he could, and pretend he wouldn't be discarded within the next few days.

WORMS

They'd come to the cabin to conceive. Carrie set herself up in the study by the porch. Sliding glass doors led outside. Sunshine broke through the trees and turned Pawpaw Lake into a mirror. She read books, preparing a women's studies class she was teaching in the fall. Her primary physician, Dr. Kniddle, said she and her husband Ben should try making love somewhere secluded, away from noisy Chicago. They rented a place in Lake County, just across the Indiana border. Her husband told her she wouldn't mellow if she brought her work with her. She said she'd be fine. The second day there, she screamed.

Her husband ran in from the kitchen. He'd been cutting vegetables for lunch. "What is it?"

She stood on a creaky wicker chair, pointing at the floor.

"Jesus," said her husband, "I hope it's not a rat." He wrenched his hands, danced like a child needing to go potty.

She pointed again.

He squinted, bent over, and put his hands on his knees. "That?" He nodded at the thick, black worm slithering across two tiles near her desk. "Jesus," he said, "it's nothing."

"Please get rid of it."

Three months before, they'd found rodent droppings in the garage. Her husband insisted they move to a new house. She'd bought a glue trap, set peanut butter in the middle of it, and carried

117

the dying rat to the trash by its tail. Yes, it was gross. But not like this, not like a *worm*.

She stepped off her chair, moved backwards. "Hurry."

"Good *Christ.*" He leaned down and picked it up with his fingers. He held it in her face, snickering.

She wanted to jump through the glass doors, run to the wooden rail along the porch, and dive into the lake. The worm didn't have rings around its body, as she expected. Its skin looked like a patchwork of mismatched, oval scales. And it was *throbbing*, getting bigger and smaller, as though it were a tiny lung. "It's disgusting," she said.

Her husband stepped closer. "This little thing?"

Without thinking about it, she slapped the bottom of his hand. The worm somersaulted through the air, arced toward her husband. She expected him to move, but he stayed still, his jaw dropped wide open. The worm flew into his mouth. He grabbed his throat and coughed.

"Oh my God," she said, "I'm *so* sorry!"

He kicked, waved his hands, knocked over one of two potted plants at the entryway to the room. He retched, he tried to spit. Nothing came out. Tears spilled down his face. He put his hand on the wall, clenched his eyes, and gulped. Once calm, he spoke in a scratchy voice. "Guess I'll finish making lunch."

She patted him on his shoulder. "I'm so sorry, sweetie." She looked at the floor to see if there were more. "Where did it come from?"

"The wood around the ceiling looks rotted. There's probably a way in for something that small."

"So there could be more?"

Initially, he shivered, grabbed his elbows. Then he straightened up, spoke in the deepest voice he could muster. "If you see another one, just let me know."

He must have forgotten the rat in the garage, or the countless times he'd screeched at mice running around their dorm room in graduate school. She'd taken care of the rodents. Least he could do was patronize her fear of worms.

* * *

After lunch, she suggested they make love. "Day sixteen," she said. She'd taken her basal temperature that morning. Ninety-seven degrees. "We got to get this train rolling."

He humped her like a child on the beach, jabbing a shovel into the sand. She said, "Let me on top." She'd read reverse cowgirl proved the most promising for conception. He reminded her that he didn't like any of those positions.

Then he squealed and rolled over. "Sorry."

"We'll try again tonight." She pulled her panties on.

"I want to do some cupping," he said. "Give me a hand?"

Cupping. An Eastern trend he'd picked up from an article on the Internet. He'd purchased a set of plastic cups from Amazon. God knows what they could have used *that* money for.

"Sure," she said. It would occupy him for fifteen minutes while she hid and finished herself. She grabbed the box of cups from a shelf in the closet. She placed two lines down either side of his spine. She pumped them until his skin stretched into mounds. Then she went into the bathroom, sat on the toilet, and imagined Denzel Washington stepping out of the shower and kneeling before her.

When she returned to the bedroom, she felt much better. She smiled at her husband, laying on his belly with the goofy cups sucking blood to the surface of his skin. She remembered the first time they'd met—*Javalution.* A coffee house on Cermak. He'd strummed slowed-down Slayer tunes on an acoustic guitar at open mic. Barely whispered the lyrics, as though they were love songs. He called it an exercise in irony. When he approached her afterwards, he used the word "ironic" so many times she lost count. But he looked non-threatening in his knit cap and purple, Northwestern scarf. It was early September. Eighty degrees, even at night. The cap and scarf, she'd assumed, represented more "irony."

The alarm clock by her side of the bed chirped. She said, "Time to take the cups off." She pulled their green nipples and removed them, up one side and down the other. Most of the rings left on his skin were pink. Toward the center of his back, however, they were darker, *black*. When she reached the middle cup, she screamed for the second time that day.

Her husband had been napping. "Turn the TV off," he said. He shook his head and finally noticed her, braced against the door to the bedroom, pointing, at his back. He craned to see. "What is it?" He sounded annoyed.

She shook her finger at him. "*Worm*."

He reached around, grazed the raised skin where the cups had been.

"Don't touch it," she said. "Come here." She started for the bathroom. There were mirrors over the sink and on the opposite wall. When he wandered in, still half awake, she turned him so he could see the reflection of his back.

"Oh," he said.

She angled for the toilet, put the lid down, and crouched on top of it. "Disgusting."

He pinched the worm with his fingers and pulled. It squirted out, along with a thin stream off blood, like a popped zit.

"Disgusting," she said again.

"Watch out." He motioned for her to get off the toilet.

"What are you doing?"

"Flushing it, what do you think?"

"What if it's diseased?"

"What if?" He held it close to her face. Unlike the worm from her workroom, this one had rings around its black skin. It was longer, skinnier.

She said, "Do you feel different?"

He scratched his ribs. "Why?"

She tried working while her husband prepared dinner. He joked, said he'd fix spaghetti to celebrate the day's "icky" discoveries. Then he said he'd make the usual—something with tofu and vegetables. God, what she'd give for a hamburger. When they started dating and he told her he was vegan, she'd thought, *Great, a beta male*. Her father was totally different. Cheated on her mother, caught herpes and chlamydia before her mother refused to sleep with him. He beat her, cracked her skull, and then moved to Canada.

Who'd chase a man across the border just for a domestic dispute? Nobody, it turned out. She'd identified herself as a feminist ever since. Swore she'd never fall for a brute.

Sometimes...*sometimes*, though, her husband tested her—he tested her patience, her tolerance for boredom, and her ability to ignore his refusal to slow down and let her relax in bed. She couldn't believe Dr. Kniddle when he said the resistance to conception came from *her* body. When she told her husband the doctor's diagnosis, he smirked.

Her extensive reading in psychoanalysis came into play: Had she knocked the worm into his mouth on purpose? Did her unconscious assume it would clog his system, make *him* responsible for their inability to have children? Or worse, would the worm avenge her mother, hand the burdens of disease right back to the males in their lives? She recalled her father sitting in the garage, preparing his tackle box before going fishing. The clumps of twisting and turning butter, peanut, and mealworms he put in the bait section. He'd drink cans of Schlitz on his boat. When he got home, he always found an excuse to yell at her and smack her mother.

"Dinner's ready," said her husband.

Thank God. No more self-evaluation. She followed him to the breakfast nook, another room overlooking the lake. He'd connected his smartphone to pink speakers she'd bought him for Christmas. His catalog of pop folk was in full swing. Hipsters singing in cutesy voices over acoustic guitars. "Could we eat in silence tonight?" she said.

"I'm feeling queasy." He grabbed his belly. "Thought the tunes might mellow my nerves."

"Whatever." She grabbed a spoonful of salad and dumped it into a wooden bowl. She picked at cut stalks of asparagus and clumps of bean sprouts. She reached for the peppershaker.

"I already seasoned it," he said.

"You never season it enough," she said.

What she could have used, right then, was a spontaneous gesture. She imagined her husband knocking the dishes to the floor, grabbing her, and laying her down on the table. The fantasy excited her, made her anxious for their love-making session later.

When she looked up, however, she didn't see Ben. She saw Dexter Cross, a running back for the Chicago Bears, gliding in and out of her at a massage-like tempo.

Her husband finished his food and rinsed his plate in the kitchen. "Think I might go to bed early." He dropped his dirty bowl in the sink for her to clean and said, "Goodnight," as though he had no intention of helping her conceive.

Sitting at the table, staring at the serving dishes and her bowl, she entertained a thought she swore she'd never consider—*divorce*. Somehow, their brief time at the cabin had revealed her husband no more sensitive than the squares on Fox News or ESPN. The faux folk music? The purple scarf? All part of a ruse. While the pigs in the world came right out and said what they wanted ("*Hey baby, let's fuck*"), men like her husband dressed metrosexual and *literally* danced around the subject. Ultimately, they utilized women the same exact way: Cook, clean, screw, rinse and repeat.

She left her dishes on the table and made her way to the bedroom. Her husband was under the covers. "Oh good," he said. "Could you turn off the lights for me?"

"Sweets?" she said.

He didn't respond.

"Excuse me?"

He sighed. "I'm here."

"Did you forget? We have to do it again."

"Oh, great." All the enthusiasm of someone in a dentist's chair awaiting a root canal. How did he even get it up for her? He kicked his covers away and slid out of his boxers. "My stomach's killing me."

She took off her jeans and t-shirt. Folded them and put them on a wooden chair near her side of the bed. She stepped out of her panties and placed them on top of a wicker nightstand. She left her bra on. Her husband hadn't played with her breasts in a year. She joked once that she'd have them "done." He'd shrugged and said, "If that makes *you* happy, go ahead and get the surgery."

Laying down next to him, she imagined making love to Paulo Tinajero, the best-looking member of the American soccer team. She ran her fingers along her husband's body and stopped. "Hey," she said.

His eyes weren't even open.

"*Hey*."

"What?"

She pointed to thin strips of his skin rising and falling across his arms, legs, and chest. "Don't you feel that?"

"Not really."

"That doesn't look healthy."

"Fine," he said. "I'll drive to Chicago and see Dr. Kniddle tomorrow."

Just like her father. He'd blow snot all over the house, bleed from his ears, vomit chunks of his insides. If her mother told him to see a doctor, he'd slap her mouth. "Stop stepping on my dick," he'd say, every time.

Her husband grabbed the back of her head and forced his tongue into her mouth. After almost choking her, he said, "Let's get you taken care of."

She wanted to scream again. The man had *never* "taken care" of her. Then she noticed his penis throbbing, the same as the worm she'd found in her study. This excited her. She sat on top of him and rocked back and forth. Normally, he'd go limp with her riding cowgirl style. Whatever the worm had done to his body, it kept him available while she rotated and shuffled until, miracle of miracles, *she* had an orgasm. She slid off him, shaking and euphoric.

He said, "Hey, I didn't get mine."

She turned her back to him and laughed. She laughed until she closed her eyes and fell asleep. She dreamed of having a daughter. Just her and her daughter, walking across a meadow in the summertime. They picked Dandelions and blew on them, scattering seeds in all directions. The world tilted. She fell into the sky.

She woke up as her head bounced off the hardwood floor. Her husband had pushed her from the bed in his sleep. She climbed to her feet, using the wicker nightstand for support. In the dark, it looked as though a four hundred-pound man had taken her husband's place. She backed toward the door to the room and flipped the light switch.

Her husband had ballooned into a mass twice his normal size. His arms, legs, and torso appeared to have been *inflated*. His skin shined, as though it were plastic. She leaned over to examine his face. His eyes stared at the ceiling, his mouth hung open. She whispered his name. No response. She shouted his name.

"Oh God," she said. She tapped his shoulder. His body exploded. Wind from the blast knocked her to the floor once more. Electricity snaked through her brain. Chunks of her husband's flesh and bones scattered and stuck to the walls and ceiling. Then a black mass of squirming worms rained down. A thousand slimy fingers grabbed her all over. They smothered her, crawled into her mouth, her nose, her ears. She bit down, crushed as many as she could with her teeth. The ones she missed slithered to her throat. She grabbed her neck, as though that might stop them.

And then the worms wiggled in between her legs.

She named the daughter she never had—*Chloe*. "Chloe," she imagined saying to the girl, "have no expectations in life. That's the only way you'll be happy." The worms burrowed into the skin above her mouth. She forced herself to smile as they wrapped themselves around her lips and squeezed.

THE PEOPLE
IN THE MARGINS

She'd been tweeting about her literature professor, Dr. Lipsek, who'd had the audacity to bring vanilla ice cream to class the day before fall break. When asked why he hadn't also provided chocolate ice cream, he'd shrugged and made a crass joke about his salary. Kayla long suspected he harbored racist tendencies. His syllabus included not one, but *two* dead white male authors. Bad enough they had to read Poe in a course called Early American Lit, but Mark Twain as well? She assumed Dr. Lipsek had swastikas painted on the walls of his apartment and, no doubt, participated in Klan rituals in Lublin. An ad popped up on the side of her twitter feed, where her hashtag *#vanillasovanilla* had already started trending in northern Indiana. "Dammit," she said. She'd installed an ad-blocker a while ago. She shouldn't have been subjected to capitalist intrusions on her activism. But she couldn't ignore the product being offered—*The Complete History of the People in the Margins*. A free e-book by "Anonymous." Good. All things should be free. Intellectual property should not be shackled by the ownership of its creator. And the people in the margins? Her specialty. She tweeted tirelessly on behalf of those less privileged. She clicked 'Accept' and minimized her browser while the new file loaded in her e-reader.

As she scanned the text, it became clear the book had nothing to do with marginalized populations. Something about a cult in nearby Pawpaw Grove. A group of early Indiana settlers who were not Protestants. The community shunned them, so they formed their own social circle. Rumors spread about their meetings on nights when the moon had achieved a particular curvature and the women of their tribe danced naked in the pale glow beaming through the Sycamores near Brandt Hollow. The locals settled for the most dubious diagnosis: witchcraft. The People in the Margins, as they'd been dubbed by their paranoid neighbors, were found one morning hanging from those same Sycamore trees. *The Lublin Free Press* ran the official story—*Mass Suicide*. Kayla had little interest in ancient tales of esoteric flirtations and the inevitable punishments they inspired. The story intrigued her from a feminist angle, however, as any hysteria over alleged witchcraft naturally would. She stretched out on her bed. Her mother must have washed the sheets. She could smell the lavender detergent her mother bought from *Family Dollar*. Human outlines formed in the spaces between the words on the virtual pages of the e-book. Initially, she dismissed them as a trick of the light. She'd painted her walls black in protest of the white shades throughout the rest of her parents' small, one-story house. As a result, the lamp overhead barely illuminated the room. She'd pinned bright posters of civil rights leaders—Beyoncé, pointing at the camera with her war face on, and Rihanna, holding an old-fashioned microphone with a cord attached to it—near the door to help create glares. She couldn't ignore the impressions of men and women in the e-book, however, their arms raised, some holding their heads, as though they were shouting, pleading for help. Had someone taken the time to typeset the e-book in such a way, done it on purpose? If she focused on the words themselves, they did not appear to be spaced in any manner different from other books. Had she gotten tired? She hadn't done anything but attend her awful lit class at Valpo, come home, eaten twice, and then set herself in front of her computer to flame Dr. Lipsek on social media. She glanced at the time on her MacBook, then at the digital alarm clock on her nightstand. Barely after midnight. She never went to sleep before two or three in the morning. The book, or the hour, or something, had messed with her mind. She closed the e-reader on her computer and opened a browser to YouTube. Any time things got too serious, she could rely on her favorite video of cats committing microaggressions.

The assembly started with her all-time favorite—a fluffy, white Persian shoving a glass off a kitchen counter despite her French Mommy (she preferred to call the owners Mommies and Daddies, to sugarcoat the obvious oppression of powerless pets) telling her, "No, no, kitty!" On a television in the background of the video, a gray image of a silhouetted woman in a pioneer bonnet blinked several times before the screen went blank again. Kayla shook her head, as though loose dirt needed jostling from her ears. She backed up the video and played it again. This time, the television behind the cat remained off. Her room, however, felt colder. Had her parents decided, right then, to do something about the environment? Had they killed the heat, thinking that would keep polar bears from falling off icebergs, like in the commercials on MTV? She rolled over and stomped through a swamp of clothes on the floor. Beating on her door, she said, "Don't be hypocrites! Turn the thermostat up!" She returned to her bed, expecting her demands to be heeded without question. She un-paused the cat video. A woman in a nice house opened the front door and placed a can of Meow Mix on top of a snow bank. Kayla grinned as the woman's cat burst through the snow near the bottom of the bank and slid across the floor. Outside the house in the video, a man in farmer's overalls held up a noose with one hand and beckoned with the index finger of his other hand. She began to resent the video. Normally a safe space, the video seemed to have been tampered with, ruining the medicine of laughter she expected it to provide. She watched the woman and the cat bursting through the snow bank again. The man with the noose did not appear. The next portion of the video involved two cats standing over an open hatch to a cellar. One smacked the other, sending it flying down the stairs. Instead of shelves filled with jarred preserves, however, a group of barely discernible people—women in bonnets, men in white shirts and black hats—stood below, glaring at the camera, *at Kayla*, as though she owed them something. She closed YouTube, leaving only twitter on the screen. As with anything disagreeable, she pretended the oddities in the video simply didn't exist.

She checked the stats on her *#vanillasovanilla* posts. Her epic, hundred-character rant about Dr. Lipsek had generated seventy-one impressions. Woke people from all over Lake County responded, most of them suggesting she find a way to get her professor fired for his insensitivity toward diverse ice cream flavors:

Chocolate aint a flavor? Can his a$$!

Bet he segregates his Neopolitan! #Racist #Chocophobia

Wut'bout caramel? 'Nana? Strwbrry? #zenafobzsux

Etc.

Additionally, many of her followers and a few strangers wondered whether Dr. Lipsek had a small penis and, thus, compensated with his biased decision to provide only vanilla ice cream in class. As Kayla 'liked' the responses she agreed with and 'blocked' anyone who defended her bigoted professor, she scanned the sides of the screen for the ad she'd clicked earlier. She hadn't paid attention to the details when she'd downloaded the e-book. Who'd published it? A Satan-worshipping press? Perhaps she'd been targeted by right-wing extremists and they'd sent her a mind-altering virus. As she dismissed her concern as paranoia, a condition only conservatives suffered, she noticed the profile avatars on the sides of the names in her twitter feed had morphed into black and white photographs of people who looked like they'd lived in the late 18th and early 19th centuries. And they were staring at her. *All of them.* "Bullshit!" she said. She hit the reload button in the navigation bar on the browser. The page recreated itself, this time with the proper profile pictures. Clearly, she'd hallucinated everything she'd seen. Maybe stress. Whatever.

Sleep came, eventually. Kayla forced thoughts of the People in the Margins from her mind by anticipating what she would find offensive in the morning when she logged back on to the Internet. If needed, she'd scour small town newspaper websites in Oklahoma or Nebraska, somewhere the deplorables were guaranteed to say or do something atrocious. She woke up much earlier than usual. Her parents hadn't yet gone to work. Gross. She flipped open her computer and scanned the trending hashtags on twitter. The first batch she checked were those with the word 'man' in them.

Chances were good they'd involve misogyny in some way. No such luck, however. She struggled to breathe. It rarely took so long to find something to induce adrenaline-seasoned indignation. Then she noticed the hashtag *#brandtshollow* in the sidebar. She closed her eyes, hoping it would not be there when she opened them. It didn't work. She clicked on it to read the tweets associated with it. A page full of black and white profile pictures loaded. The tweets appeared to be from residents of Pawpaw Grove:

If thee feels kin toward none but God, ye may breathe easy

Let ye who challenge the Almighty meet thine maker soon

Yay, shall the Lord's enemies in Pawpaw be smote

Etc.

Every other tweet included an emoji resembling an empty noose. Kayla drew back from the screen. The icon for her e-reader blinked underneath the browser. She clicked on it and the e-book reappeared. "Enough," she said. She navigated into the top menu and deleted the e-book from her computer. She clicked on the trashcan icon and emptied it. As soon as the title, *The People in the Margins*, disappeared from her screen, her shoulders shook. Her mother taught her that meant someone had walked on her grave. She knew better. She knew it somehow represented patriarchal oppression, materializing in her physical well being. Then she noticed her poster of Rihanna on her wall had changed. The microphone in her hand had become a noose. Kayla turned away, refused to consider whether she'd hallucinated the rope. She stared at the only window in her room. Outside, an oak, its leaves browning for autumn, wrapped its imposing branches around her side of the house. She'd climbed them a hundred times as a little girl. Somewhere in puberty, when she'd asked her dad to stop tucking her in before bed, she'd put on weight and could no longer hoist herself onto even the lowest branches. Until now, the tree had never looked threatening. When she glanced back at the poster, Rihanna's hand grasped a microphone once more. "Quit being paranoid," said Kayla. "Next thing you know, you'll be voting republican." Her mother and father clanked dishes and silverware in the kitchen. Her stomach made monster noises. She closed the computer, changed into jeans and a t-shirt with the words *Pussy*

Power on it, grabbed her smartphone off her desk, and trudged out of her room and down the dark hallway leading to the pleasing scent of bacon and eggs.

Her father, dressed for his job at Third Bank and Trust in Merrillville, sat on his side of the table, his newspaper next to his plate. *Wall Street Journal.* Goddamn fascist. Her mother shuffled around the kitchen, scraping food from a pan onto her plate and asking her father if he needed more. When she saw Kayla, her eyes popped. "Snookums!" she said. "What are you doing up so early?" She put the pan and spatula on the stove and wiped her hands on her red and white-checkered apron. She'd tied her hair in a bun with a loose end bouncing when she walked. "It's been so long since we've seen you at breakfast." She pulled eggs from a carton on the counter next to the stove and cracked them over the pan. "Looks like I'll have to get more bacon!" She glided across the linoleum floor like an ice skater.

"Hungry so soon?" The morning sun beamed in behind her father, turning his balding scalp yellow. He had to be the last man on Earth who wore suspenders instead of a belt.

"What's that supposed to mean?" said Kayla.

Her father looked up from his paper, gave her the same aggressive, condescending stare he'd assaulted her with her entire life. "You had two full plates for dinner last night."

"Mom…"

Her mother peeled the plastic off of bacon she'd retrieved from the freezer.

"Mom!" said Kayla. "He's fat-shaming me again!"

"Fat-shaming?" Her father howled. "What did I tell you about bringing that gobbledygook into my house?"

"It's not your…"

"Not only do I put the bread on the table, young lady," he said, "I pay your tuition as well. And for what? You're majoring in cultural studies. How is that even a thing?"

"MOM!"

Her mother waved a limp hand at them. "Play nice, you two."

"What are you going to do with your degree?" Her father would *not* stop bullying her. "Once you land a solid minimum wage job at Starbucks, will you move out then? No, I'm sure I'm going to be supporting you for the rest of my life. Good luck when I'm dead."

Oh, how she *hated* that man. She wanted to berate him, tell him, for the hundredth time, she'd go to graduate school and get a Masters in education. A reasonable plan, dammit. In the bright light obscuring the frame on the picture window behind her father, dark impressions of people gathered. They looked like an army, there to support her father's dated, patriarchal mansplaining. He said something else about food, something like, "Might as well keep eating, keep the fridge clear for your mother."

"Jesus!" She hated using a Judeo-Christian reference in a moment requiring strength. It slipped out. Her parents went to church, she didn't. She'd lectured her mother constantly about compromising, about being a strong, intelligent woman, independent of the church's misogynist claws. Her mother only scoffed, told her she didn't feel the need to stir up any controversy in her marriage. "I'll get breakfast at the mall," said Kayla. She stomped into the hallway, grabbed her *Indiana ACLU* windbreaker from the coat closet. She rummaged through her mother's purse, took her car keys, popped the button on her wallet, and grabbed two twenties. Her father lumbered behind her, hooking his thumbs in his suspenders.

"You think you can just mouth off and leave without an explanation?" Behind his voice, whispers, like ghosts, filled the house. "Young lady?"

Young lady. If she could knee the old man in his crotch, she would. She didn't want to touch him, though. Didn't like him being anywhere near her. She sucked in her belly and snaked around him.

"I'm talking to you," he said.

"Drop dead." She slammed the front door as she left.

Normally, she'd go to the mall on I-65, situated between Haggard and Lublin. Most of the people who shopped there were poor, reminded her of her own family. Her mother and father had fallen for the oldest trick in the book—they voted republican and slaved for pathetic paychecks, expecting their heroes in Washington D.C.

to pass magical legislation turning all those who "worked hard" and "did the right thing" into millionaires. She drove the extra fifteen miles to Valpo, instead. Maybe she'd run into friends from her women's studies classes. She hadn't found anything particularly juicy to get upset over in the morning news, but she could recycle the outrage her lit professor had caused. She parked near the JCPenney and went inside. Her anger subsided in the bright aisles of the ancient capitalist temple. Muzak, dripping like syrup from the speakers in the ceiling, reminded her of being younger, going clothes shopping with her mother the day after Christmas, when everything got marked down by at least fifty percent. She'd been her parents' little angel then—slim, pretty (according to the standards of the ridiculous patriarchy), *compliant*. At Easter, she'd sit on the knee of a man in a bunny costume in the middle of the mall and smile on command. As her body developed in the sixth grade, her father constantly wanted to tickle her. When she told her mother she didn't like the way he tucked her in at night, her mother accused her of having an active imagination. They hadn't spoken in any meaningful, intimate manner since. Now she bought her own clothes with her allowance. Usually at Goodwill. She liked going to shops in the mall, however, like Hot Topic, and pretending she could afford the fashionable protest gear her rich antifa friends from Chicago wore.

As she strolled across the polished tile, trying to identify the geezer song transmogrified by the Muzak, shadows scampered behind the racks of clothes. Hints of people ducked any time she tried to focus on them. The women wore bonnets, like settlers in pioneer times (or whatever reactionary history books referred to that murderous period as), and the men wore suspenders (must be the choice accessory of the oppressor) and hats similar to those she'd seen in documentaries on the Amish. There were Amish communities in Indiana. Possible they'd taken a walk to Valpo to do some shopping. Their refusal to let her get a good look at them annoyed her. Then it alarmed her. Memories of the e-book she'd read the night before trickled through her thoughts. She stepped into the maternity section, chasing after a pair of women she could have sworn had giggled and pointed at her. She rounded a rack of blue dresses with expanded midsections for pregnant women and stopped. A slender high school boy with a split brow over his left eye stood near the dressing rooms and smiled at her. Was this some loser, couldn't get a date with a girl his age? Thought he might be doing her a favor by giving her attention? The boy ran his eyes up and down her. His nametag identified him as *Victor*. He spoke with a hint of a Mexican or Latino accent (how was she supposed to know the difference?). He said, "Looks like you're just about due, yes?"

"Excuse me?"

"Your baby," he said, "looks like it's about to spring from the oven, yes?" He held his arms behind his back and smiled and nodded. Too much. As though he were appropriating Asian culture for no legitimate reason.

She rolled her neck like an outraged African-American woman on *Jerry Springer*—"I am *not* pregnant!"

The boy put his hand over his mouth and smirked. He composed himself and said, "I'm sorry, ma'am."

"Ma'am?" She sucked in air and made herself bigger. "I doubt I'm even five years older than you."

Now the boy had the nerve to look as though *he* had been slighted. "I made a mistake, lady, jeez." He slunk back to the checkout desk and sorted through clothes on a table behind the register.

Kayla forced herself to walk through the *JC Penney* without acknowledging the people hiding behind the racks. She obsessed over the amazingly offensive thing the boy had said. *Pregnant.* Really? Like she would ever be dumb enough to perpetuate the human tragedy. If she had a boyfriend, she'd make him wear a condom. And she'd be on the pill. And she'd get that shot, Depo-Provera. Her sexually active friends told her to build as much of a wall as possible to keep filthy man-juice from her eggs. She passed the cookie stand, told herself to pretend it didn't exist. She knew better, though. She'd grab breakfast at the food court and then buy a giant-sized, double-stuffed Oreo pie to eat on the way home. She wandered into the *Hot Topic* to see if they'd gotten any new band t-shirts she could imagine wearing at the next campus protest, whenever it might be and whatever it might be against. Obnoxious rock music played on the speakers. Pretty atavistic, if they'd asked her. Rock bands were meant to be thought of as relics, worshipped by wearing their logos on clothes. Not listened to, though. If it didn't have a hip-hop beat denoting protected classes, it couldn't be called music. Not in the twenty-first century. The store reeked of jasmine incense. An anorexic girl with pink hair and more piercings in her ears than Kayla had in her entire body stood on the riser in the center. She had her iPhone in her face until Kayla cleared her throat.

"Oh," said the girl. She put her phone on the glass display counter. "What's up?"

"I was here last Thursday," said Kayla. "Have you gotten any new t-shirts, you know, with old bands on them?"

"Ooh." The girl pressed her bone-skinny finger to her cute, dimpled chin. "I don't know." She stepped down from behind the display cases. "Let's take a look." She motioned with her arm for Kayla to follow her. They wound through the dimly lit store, past collector's toys and lava lamps and other trinkets designed, no doubt, to make lonely stoners feel better about themselves, to a wall of t-shirts with a giant sign at the top announcing, *Big and Beautiful!* "Let's see," said the girl. She craned her head, scanning each column of designs. "I think that's a new Nirvana print." She pointed at a shirt the size of a tent adorned with a photo of Kurt Cobain picking his nose with his middle finger.

"Why'd you bring me *here*?" said Kayla.

The twig played dumb. She set her finger on her chin again, as though looking precious would erase her assumptive, fat-shaming gesture. "T-shirts?" She said it as though she'd never heard the word.

Kayla nodded at the *Big and Beautiful!* sign. "You just *assume* I wear a larger size?"

Two young African-American women entered the store. They stopped at a dual-display of 2Pac and Notorious B.I.G. memorabilia. The sales clerk spoke to Kayla in a quiet voice. "Excuse me, just a minute." She hustled over to the hip-hop merchandise near the register. To the African-American women, she said, "Can I help you?" Not in the tone she'd used when greeting Kayla, rather, impatient and distressed.

"Just browsing," said one of the women.

"Okay." The girl held her wrists behind her back and stood next to them.

Kayla had seen enough. She marched to the counter and said, "I think I need to speak with your boss."

The sales clerk and the women looked at her.

"*You*," she said to the sale clerk. "You obviously have a problem with African-Americans."

The girl drew in her face, as though she'd smelled something rotten.

One of the African-American women made a similar expression. "She ain't bothering nobody, *fatass*."

Both of the women broke out in hysterics. Even in the dim lighting, Kayla could see the sales girl blushing, trying to hold in her laughter. She pushed past the three of them and charged out into the open air of the mall. She wanted to cry. Every single incident like that reminded her of the first time she'd heard someone refer to her in terms of her weight. She'd been in the eighth grade. For two years, she'd spent her allowance on Suzy Qs and had gained over a hundred pounds. She'd been sent to the principal's office for clobbering Billy Barnes with her textbook in math class. He'd called her *Cheese Breath*. The secretary in the office had announced her to the principal—"Kayla Pugh, ma'am. Fighting. Again." The principal had said, in a voice she probably thought wouldn't carry, "You mean the chubby girl?" An adult, a *female* adult, no less, unable to find a kinder way to describe her, had driven home the reality that she no longer looked like a Barbie doll, that she would have to scrap for the things she wanted in life because boys only liked skinny girls. She'd burst into tears that day and decided, after being suspended by the principal, she would never allow anyone to control her emotions ever again. She pulled up her nose and threw her shoulders forward, walked like a boss to the food court. She headed straight for the A&W stand, for a burger, fries, and a large root beer with light ice. She continued seeing blurs in the corners of her eyes—gray, diminutive figures, like shadows. Before she could get to the A&W counter and order, however, someone called her name. She turned, expecting to see an old pioneer, maybe his face rotting, worms crawling from empty eye-sockets, telling her the biggest mistake she'd ever made was downloading the e-book and then erasing it from her computer.

"Kayla?"

She heard it again. She spun all the way around and stepped backwards. Her disgusting *Early American Lit* professor, Dr. Lipsek, stood near the Panda Express with a plate of steaming broccoli in his hands. A shiver ran through her body. For whatever reason, the man reminded her of her father. He didn't look or sound like him—Dr. Lipsek couldn't be more than thirty-five or thirty-six. He stood like a frail hunchback (would that offend people with deformed spines? *Shit...*), wore spectacles, and probably hadn't washed or cut his hair since the Bush administration. Her father would have called him a liberal fruitcake, but she knew better— Dr. Lipsek was a Nazi. His inability to provide diverse ice cream flavors to his students had proven it. "Oh," she said. "Hello..."

"You think I don't have a twitter account?"

Maybe she blushed. She couldn't tell. Her face certainly *felt* warmer. She didn't respond, however.

He set the tray with his plate of vegetables on the counter. "You can't just slander me on social media and think you're going to get away with it."

"I don't know what you're talking about." She avoided eye-contact.

"I saw the hashtag, saw your name on the initial tweet. You called me a fascist. I'm not Italian, Kayla. Do you even *know* what a fascist is? Later, you called me a Grand Wizard. Never mind that I've been a staunch leftist since before you were born. Libelous comments like that can get me fired."

"Good." She slapped her hand over her mouth as soon as she said it.

"Well..." He stepped closer, stared down at her from his thin, Himmler-like spectacles. "I've already spoken with the dean. We're going to meet with your advisor when the break ends and decide whether or not you should be allowed to continue attending Valpo." He smiled, reminded her of the judge in the *Roger Rabbit* movie, picked up his tray, and walked to a table in the middle of the food court. His posture improved, as though dropping his patriarchal weight on her, adding to the oppression she'd already been dealt in life, had made him stronger. As he sat down, people in pioneer clothes gathered around him. They crossed their arms and glared at Kayla.

Her heart thundered. She didn't have panic attacks often. Any time she felt one coming on, she looked on her phone or her computer for something to be offended by and that would distract her long enough to wiggle out of her own head. Food also provided relief from anxiety. But the people in the margins, or the people who'd hanged them, she couldn't tell which were which, were *everywhere*. She ran back through the mall, past the *Hot Topic*, past the cookie stand, through the *JC Penney*, out the door and to her car. She jammed the key into the ignition and tuned the radio to NPR. Someone with a British accent bemoaned the lack of diversity at a Celtic dance performance she'd recently attended in Ireland. Between the woman's soothing, chamomile voice and the air blowing through the vents, Kayla managed to slow down her heart. She put the car in drive and headed home. Her parents, hopefully, would be off to their horrible jobs and she'd have the house to herself.

She pulled into the driveway and shut off the car. On the way to the front door, she stopped and considered the tree outside her bedroom window. All the evil people in the world who fat-shamed her would no doubt insist she couldn't climb the branches if she tried. She approached the old oak, put her hands on its rough bark. She grabbed the limb closest to the ground and struggled to pull herself up. Her arms burned and her hands felt as though someone scraped her palms with a razor blade. She dropped to the ground and looked around, nervous her neighbors might have seen her embarrassing attempt. She needed to find something to be offended by, and quick. The day, so far, had been so rotten, had reminded her of everything she hated about life. She thought, for the first time since being introduced to the medicine of indignation, about killing herself. Such fancies were a problem in high school. Her parents had sacrificed money they'd saved for vacations to send her to a psychiatrist. Of course, the pervert had wanted her to talk about sex and he put her on pills that made her head spin. The moment she learned to worry about people less privileged than her, she no longer required antidepressants or the manipulative shrink.

Once inside the house, she found a note her father had taped to her bedroom door. The patriarchal bastard scolded her for taking her mother's car on a day she needed it to go to work. Whatever. Like the selfish prick couldn't give her a ride? She felt a little better, finding someone very *real* to be angry at. She crumpled the note as she entered her room and tossed it into a *Wonder Woman* wastebasket by her desk. She flipped her computer open and logged on to the Internet. The sight of the political hashtags on the sidebar of her twitter page worked better than psychotropic drugs. Her blood calmed. How stupid had she been, entertaining ancient fantasies of suicide? How could she battle oppression if she were dead? She almost—*almost*—felt guilty for being so insensitive. Such transgressions had to be the result of psychic coercion by the patriarchy. As she scrolled down the slew of news stories worthy of getting offended by, a chill ran through her. She looked around her room. The air whispered, though she couldn't discern what it had said. When she returned her gaze to her MacBook, the screen had gone blank. She smacked the back of it, then lowered it, thinking it may have blinked out, temporarily. Through the window, she saw a group of women in bonnets and men in black-rimmed hats gathered around the tree outside, staring at her.

She snapped the curtains on her window closed. Her mother had sewn them for her when she was a little girl. They were thin, flimsy, and the silhouettes of the people seemed to close in on her. She clenched her eyes and saw the very same crowd of settlers, moving toward her in the darkness of her thoughts. The panic resurfaced. Her breathing staggered. She turned away from the window and opened her eyes. Beyoncé, the Queen of All Things Relevant, no longer pointed at the camera in the poster on Kayla's wall. Her fierce, patriarchy-battling finger now jabbed to her right, toward the window. Kayla swiveled in her chair, back to the curtains. She stood and drew them. The silhouettes had vanished. Hanging from a branch halfway up the tree, a noose swayed in the light, autumn wind. Only one idea occupied her mind: She would go outside and she would climb that damn tree. She would show everyone, *especially* her father, that she could do anything she wanted.

Alec Cizak is a writer and filmmaker from Indiana. His published books include *Down on the Street* and *Breaking Glass*. He is also the editor of the fiction journal *Pulp Modern*.

Made in the
USA
Lexington, KY